I0612257

BOOKS BY OLIVIA ASH

Nighthelm Academy

City of the Sleeping Gods

City of Fractured Souls

City of the Enchanted Queen

Demon Queen Saga

Princes of the Underworld

Wars of the Underworld

Mistress of the Underworld

Sentinel Saga

By Dahlia Leigh and Olivia Ash

The Shadow Shifter

The Demon Prince

The Rogue Alchemist

STAY CONNECTED

Olivia Ash occasionally takes over the Wispvine Publishing social media channels on Facebook, Instagram, and Twitter. She also has her own Facebook page.

Olivia also likes to hang out with Lila Jean in their Facebook group specifically for readers like you to come together and share their lives and interests, especially regarding the hot guys from their reverse harem novels. Please check it out and join in whenever you get the chance! Everyone in there is amazing, and you'll fit right in.

https://www.facebook.com/groups/LilaJeanOliviaAsh/

Sign up for email alerts of new releases AND exclusive access to bonus content, book recommendations, and more!

https://wispvine.com/newsletter/demon-queen-saga-email-signup/

Enjoying the series? Awesome! Help others discover the Nighthelm Academy by leaving a review at Amazon.

WARS OF THE UNDERWORLD

BOOK TWO OF THE DEMON QUEEN SAGA

OLIVIA ASH

CONTENTS

CHAPTER ONE

SADIE

*S*adie looked out over her land from Steele's balcony while sipping champagne and wistfully smiling to herself. For the first time since arriving in Bitterthorn, she was happy and at peace.

She could never get enough of the endless arrays of trees and shrubs that covered a land she would have once thought barren. It truly was like her own little paradise.

The way this place mirrored the world above never ceased to amaze her. Especially the trillions of tiny, colorful crystals that glowed depending on the time of day. It was easy to confuse the sunset of her world in comparison to the one above, as there wasn't actually a sun in the underworld. And the one here in the underworld was so much better. The colors were much more vivid and deeper, brighter.

The magic was constantly enchanting. Everything thrummed with it—with her—and she even felt her connection with the fortress growing stronger as each day passed.

As she took in all the hills, trees, cliffs, and beautiful, star-like crystals that coated the ceiling of the underworld, she thought about all of the things she had gained in such a short amount of time.

And it's all mine!

For starters, she was powerful beyond her wildest dreams. She was loved by four amazing demon princes. And she was *queen*.

Swords clanging against each other echoed to her, drawing her attention to Mordecai and Kaiser sparring in the courtyard below. They moved wickedly fast, almost turning into a blur Sadie could barely keep up with. It seemed they were equally matched against each other as Mordecai shifted to shadow and Kaiser somehow predicted where Mordecai would shift back. They tumbled to the ground, wrestling and laughing. Some of the laughter bubbled up to where Sadie stood, and she couldn't help but chuckle.

Damien, she was sure, was off doing his own thing while Steele still slept in bed.

She glanced over her shoulder at his exposed chest and the sheet that barely covered his groin. Her heart swelled, and she sighed in bliss.

The peaceful moment was only a break between wars. Sadie knew that deep down. So, she absorbed every ounce of tranquility she could get in the time she could.

It had been about a month since Zagan, the demon king, stood right inside her front gate and demanded that she ally with him. He also threatened war if she chose any of his sons.

Well, she chose all four. That decision would do very little in the way of pleasing the princes' father, which would bring his promised conflict.

With her magic and her fortress, Sadie felt capable to fight whatever war he would bring to her, especially with her men at her side. But first things first—she needed to amass an army of her own beyond her fiery ifrits. Too many of them had been sacrificed to war as it was, and she didn't want to lose anymore than that. The last group of ifrits Hobson had sent out never returned, leaving Sadie to assume the worst.

Two groups killed by Mara.

At least the demoness wasn't a problem anymore.

A shadow darted across the horizon, zig-zagging through the shrubbery, inching ever closer to the fortress but never coming quite close. There had been a lot of those things over the past few days edging nearer to her land. She wondered what sort of creature it was. She knew better than to think it wasn't a scout, likely working for that wretched demon king. That would be the type of move Zagan would make. A tactic to gauge how powerful she was becoming.

And that reminded her, with little to no time left, Zagan would come knocking down her door again. Though Sadie hoped her decision wouldn't lead to a war with Zagan, she knew, deep down in her being, the demon king would show up. Likely in another show of force, he would try to destroy everything she had built. She just needed to defeat him before it came to that. That shadowy creature only signaled a means to an end. A reason to train harder, gain more allies, and further cement her claim to her throne.

But how do you defeat an immortal demon king, and one as powerful as Zagan?

Sadie was only a human from the world above. A place where most people didn't believe demons, let alone demon kings, existed. Had she not have been given the amulet by Blair, her sister, she would prob-ably still be working long days as a trained paramedic, living alone, and having not much of a social life to speak of. Now, she was queen of a land far more majestic than she could have ever dreamt. If it weren't for Hobson, Damien, Kaiser, Steele, and Mordecai, she wouldn't have had a clue on what it meant to be queen, much less how to kill a demon king.

She knew she should talk to them about the

upcoming war, especially with Zagan's own sons, but she needed to first think about defenses.

Sadie went to her room and crossed the floor to her own balcony. She stared at the gates in front of her fortress. She scanned the shadows, looking for anything that would suggest weaknesses as she wondered what could be done to refortify her fortress's defenses.

As queen, it was her duty to protect what's hers, and she would do whatever it took to do so.

She became lost in thought. And the ideas that ran through her mind created a churning, chaotic mess of emotions. The small of her back warmed. She felt eyes on her.

Turning, she found all four men staring at her expectantly.

"Are you all right?" Kaiser asked. His eyebrows had knitted themselves together.

Sadie propped a hand on her hip.

What is so hard about 'stay out of my room?' I need privacy. I need time alone*!*

Taking in a deep breath, she had to appreciate that they always somehow knew when she was in a bad mood.

Oh, my stupid, incessant, ridiculously adorable men.

Their continuous need to interrupt her privacy was likely never going to end. Even though she still demanded her alone time, and they continuously ignored the rule about not barging into her chamber, she couldn't stay mad at them. Perhaps she should accept the inevitable.

She didn't yet, though. Privacy was important to her, and she needed time to be alone and to think. She couldn't very well do that with one of the princes constantly looking over her shoulder.

Regardless, she let go of wanting to berate them for their antics and smiled at them.

"I'm fine. I was just thinking." She narrowed her eyes on them. "How do you always seem to know when something is troubling me? You show up at just the right moments."

The men exchanged glances, shifting their weight from one foot to the next.

Kaiser said, "Never mind about that. What was troubling you?"

She took in a deep breath and slowly let it out through pursed lips. "I was thinking of the fortifications that surround this fortress. I wonder what is in place, other than vines, to keep unwanted guests out."

The men stared in varying degrees of apprehension at her.

Kaiser said, "I don't think that's it."

"Well, you'll have to deal with that. We need to fortify the barrier. The last time it was attacked, too many enemies filtered through. If your father were to show up with a heavy force, the barrier wouldn't stand a chance. Vines won't be enough to stop him and his army from entering the fortress."

Steele yawned and scratched his head. "What happened to relaxing? Or are you always all work and no play?"

Sadie shook her head. "There is a time and place for relaxing. I just happened to have thought about your father coming soon, and I want to be prepared."

Reaching into her connection with the fortress, she summoned Hobson. And like clockwork, the gargoyle appeared within a few seconds, ready and willing to do her bidding. She quickly thought of giving him a vacation but dismissed it for the moment. She had a job for him.

"Please check the barrier for weak spots and do what you can to reinforce them. I don't want any vulnerable areas that could get exploited."

He nodded. "Of course, Sadie. I don't sense any weak areas, but it could be worth pursuing closer if it would please and reassure her Majesty."

"Better to be safe than sorry." She paused and added, "Can you come up with a way to add additional reinforcements to the barrier? At this rate, we'll need several layers of protection around the fortress."

Sadie had yet to fight Zagan, or any demon king for that matter, but she sure as hell knew it would take a lot of fire power and protective barriers to repel him.

"I will see what I can do," Hobson said.

She turned to her men and said, "I would appreciate your help in doing the same. It's important we remain protected against further surprise attacks and prevent any more breaches onto my land."

Each of them nodded, saying they would do so following dinner.

"Which will be ready in about an hour," Hobson said. "Will there be anything else, my queen?"

"No, thank you."

He nodded, and everyone followed him out the door to the dining hall.

Once Sadie slipped out of the door, she pulled Mordecai by the arm to stop him. He settled his gaze on her and a crease formed between his eyebrows.

"Maybe you could do something for me beyond reinforcing the barrier. I need you to make sure no one else can get into the fortress the same way you had."

The memory of how they met floated through her mind, and she smiled. Once she got to know him a little more, he showed her his shadow form and demonstrated his ability to infiltrate even her own fortress's defenses.

A wicked smile stretched his lips and he nodded.

"Anything, for you." He kissed her once then rejoined his brothers.

Satisfied for at least a plan to amp the defenses of her home, she continued to the dining hall, ready for dinner.

CHAPTER TWO

SADIE

*T*he laughter was contagious. Sadie and her men enjoyed an extravagant dinner with foods she had only dreamt of. Being queen certainly had its perks, and lavish food was one of them. The spreads looked expensive and were colorful. Sadie could only guess what they were, but each of the servings she had were so full of flavor, she couldn't get enough.

She watched as the brothers teased and poked fun at each other.

"Mordecai, you've gotten soft in your time here. I was never able to catch you like I did earlier this morning," Kaiser said before letting out a chuckle.

Mordecai smirked and nonchalantly shrugged his shoulders. "I still spanked you with my shadow sword."

Kaiser stopped laughing. "It still hurts, you know."

Steele's eyes lit up in response to the story of the sparring match that occurred while he slept. "I must say, I'm rather disappointed I missed out on the fun. I imagine it would've been better two against one."

Sadie asked, "Is that a challenge, Steele? Are you sure you can handle both of them at once?"

Steele smiled, smug and self-assured. "I, my dear, can handle much, much more."

"There he goes, switching the topic to something sex related," Damien said. "Do you guys remember when he first came into his power?" He shook his head, waving his hand in front of him as he choked back a fit of laughter. "The servants wouldn't go near him for months!"

The demon princes erupted in a fit of laughter. Sadie giggled as she imagined a newly maturing Steele coping with his sexual desires. Horn dog didn't seem like a term that would fit.

Kaiser said between bouts of laughter, "He humped everything in sight." He gasped for air and tried to form words between his spurts of hilarity. Eventually, he gave up, wiping a tear that had fallen down his cheek.

"I seem to recall you being a bit slow on the maturation as far as demons go, Kaiser," Steele said, dark and lethal. "Shall we share in those embarrassments?"

He snorted. "What embarrassments?"

"What about that time when you had your first kill?" Mordecai offered.

All the brothers lost control of themselves again.

Sadie sipped on her champagne, really loving the way the men were getting along. Though she adored spending time with her men individually, she felt like she had a true family when they spent time *together*.

"I've seen you all do some pretty ridiculous things," Damien said, twirling a knife in his hand with a foot propped up in his chair. His other arm was draped over his knee. His deep blue eyes settled on Sadie's for a moment, setting her body on fire.

Mordecai sat up in his chair, leaning over the table with his fingers folded together as he said, "Oh yeah? Curious, brother, pray tell."

She finished the last of her dinner and downed the final drop of champagne before standing. All the laughter stopped. Everyone turned their attention toward her.

Okay, so there are things I still need to get used to.

She cleared her throat. "I'm going to train. Feel free to continue having your fun, but please don't forget your promise to check the barrier." Her gaze met Mordecai's, a silent reminder to explore the castle grounds in smoke form—and to make sure he was the only one who could.

"Wouldn't dream of it," Kaiser said and stood.

Steele rose to his feet as well, approaching her and

leaving a kiss on her hand. "Won't you stay a while longer, Captain? Or are you truly all work and no play?" He winked.

Sadie couldn't stop the chuckle that left her lips if she tried. "No, Steele. I need to train. We all should, as much as possible."

"Will you need my assistance, Your Majesty?" Hobson asked, leaving his perch by the wall, having observed the evening shenanigans in his quiet way.

She shook her head. "No, thank you, Hobson. I'll be training *alone* tonight." She pointedly looked at each of the princes, whom she hoped would be taking the word alone to heart. Then again, she really needed to consider a private place to train, somewhere the men couldn't impose themselves on. But that would have to wait.

All things in good time.

SADIE

Sadie stared at the horizon, covered in sweat as she finished a downward strike of her shadow sword. The air chilled her skin as she moved in rhythm to a faded memory of a tune in her mind. She loved pushing herself harder each time she trained. She grew stronger, even more powerful, and it felt good.

Something was coming. And soon. Something very, very bad.

A scratch clawed at her mental barrier.

Well, he wasn't watching, but technically still interrupting. She debated on whether to let him in or not. Then the scratch came with a little more begging. She sighed and let Steele in.

An image of one of the halls in the lower parts of her fortress filled her mind. Then his voice followed.

"I found a barely visible weak area in the fortifications here." He pointed at the area. Sadie couldn't really tell the difference, but she took Steele's word for it. She was more shocked that he could actually speak to her in her mind.

Neat.

"I'm going to refortify this and add a few extra layers of a ward."

She wondered if she should respond to him. After all, it wasn't like a telephone, was it?

"Oh, and here's something 'neat'..."

Steele flooded her mind with images of the chained shackles on the brick wall, her naked body strapped to them, and him doing wickedly delicious things to her.

Sadie shook her head and refocused on her training. At least she knew for certain Steele could hear her thoughts. First with the music and their little dance, and now this.

She gave Steele a mental nudge to let him know he could "disconnect." She had practice to finish. She swung her sword in front of her, crisscrossing from left to right. That feeling of foreboding continued to increase. The longer she practiced, the more she felt it. Her senses were set on high alert. Warning raged through her veins.

The lights from the colorful crystals covering the ceiling of the underworld deepened to dark blues and purples and then to deep navy, silver, and gold. Red crystals scattered themselves ever so often. The red slowly faded into the horizon.

She continued to practice, knowing she needed to be well prepared in case Zagan decided to rear his ugly head before she had time to procure an army. And she found comfort in knowing her men were out following her orders in finding weaknesses within the ground's fortifications. Hobson as well.

Slashing her shadow sword to the left, and to the right, she halted mid-step as she went to jab in front of her. Someone just walked onto her land. Her nerves tingled, and the hair on the back of her neck rose.

She turned around, letting go of her shadow sword, finding Hobson approaching.

"Who is interrupting my training now?" she asked and wiped sweat from her brow.

"My apologies, Your Highness, but it appears the angel, Evangeline, is here.

Wonderful. Not just any angel, but that *one.*

She sighed. Though weary of losing allies, she couldn't afford to make more enemies, either. Besides, maybe a couple of angels were just what she needed in her arsenal of ass-kicking creatures.

"Very well. Let her know that I will be a moment. I need to clean up. I'll meet her in the throne room."

"As you wish, Your Highness," Hobson said and hurried off.

Of course, she wouldn't hurry. Instead, she would take her time getting cleaned up... not to mention adding a dagger or two to her outfit just in case the angel wanted to try anything.

The first time she had met Evangeline, Sadie was less than pleased. All her original conceptions of what it meant to be an angel were thrown out the window the moment she spoke. The princes had warned her they were not all glitter, love, and light. And Evangeline was the furthest thing from any semblance of a benign, sweet creature from up above.

She may be forced to play host to the angel again, but that didn't mean she had to do it the moment her arrival was announced. Queens were busy, and she wanted to take her time preparing to face the angel.

An exhausting encounter this would more than likely be.

CHAPTER THREE

SADIE

*S*adie took her time and showered. After all, why not remind the angel of who she was dealing with? She even dressed in a long black dress with a plunging neckline. It accented her pendant perfectly with the lines of ink that still swirled along her chest, looking more like thorns now instead of wavy lines.

By the time she made it downstairs and to the foyer, Damien was there. He and Evangeline seemed to have finished a tense exchange of words. Hobson stood to the side. When Sadie looked at him, he shrugged.

"I tried to tell her, Your Majesty—"

"I am not here to see you," Evangeline said, rather bluntly and to the point.

Damien sighed and faced Sadie. "I asked her here on a favor."

Evangeline snorted.

Sadie raised an eyebrow. "A favor?"

Damien nodded. "My alliance with the angels is tense, at best. But Evangeline is a damn good scout, and I asked that she keep an eye out for the group of ifrits that have yet to come ba—"

"They're dead." Evangeline's words felt like a punch to Sadie's gut.

Sadie shifted her gaze to the angel who stood as though it was of no consequence that some of her people were indeed dead. She wasn't sure if she wanted to break down and cry or wring the angel's neck for being so callous toward her loss. They were still lives lost. Weren't angels supposed to revere all life?

"Toughen up, demon queen, lest your soft heart be seen as weakness." She narrowed her eyes on Sadie then sighed and shook her head. "Still can't see how you are human in appearance."

"I'll take your words under advisement." *For all of about five seconds.*

But Sadie had no intention of exchanging compassion for cruelty. She may have been demon queen, but that didn't make her demonic. A demon-human hybrid. Though she still had yet to figure out what that meant for her or how that came to be, it didn't change the fact she would hang on to her values—the human values she grew up with and made her who she was. She wasn't like Hecate. She liked to think that her politeness and gentle heart was what set her apart from the previous demon queen.

The confirmation of more fallen ifrits strengthened Sadie's resolve to not call on them in battles to come. They were loyal and served her well, but she refused to treat them like expendable fodder. And after the loss of some of her best ifrits to the evil demoness, Mara, she hated the idea of causing their numbers to dwindle.

Evangeline shifted, drawing Sadie's attention to her again. "It wasn't so much by Damien's request that I'm here, but because of your predecessor, Hecate. We watched her commit numerous evils with audacity, and now we're watching you. I'm here to make sure you aren't repeating the same mistakes. Apparently, the other angels are leery about another demon queen." She sighed as if bored. "They don't want to involve themselves unless absolutely necessary. And let me warn you, they will if they believe you are going down the same path as Hecate."

Damien stepped between them, his eyes glinting dangerously. "I don't like what you are implying here. Threatening my woman isn't a good way to keep this alliance going."

Evangeline shrugged. "Don't shoot the messenger. I

have a job to do, and because I had to check in on the progress Sadie made, I did that little favor for you as a kindness." She cocked her head to the side. "You really should be grateful, as I don't often lend favors to demons. Had it not been for our alliance, for what it is worth, I wouldn't have wasted my time on you."

Sadie wondered what horrors Hecate had done to be hated by so many. She knew she inherited not only Hecate's power but her enemies as well when she became queen. Though it would take some time to show the creatures in her new realm that she was different from the previous demon queen, she only had a matter of time before they all came knocking at her gate, demanding her head.

Exactly like Zagan.

She took a deep breath, rubbing her forehead. *One problem at a time.*

Yes, Hecate was a possible threat, but Zagan was the one that needed to be addressed immediately.

"What do you know about Zagan?" she asked the angel.

Evangeline shifted her cold gaze to Sadie. "Not involved. But good luck with that." Her words came out very sarcastic. Her voice turned sickeningly sweet as she faced Damien. "Anything else?"

Damien growled.

The angel narrowed her eyes on him and sighed. "Very well. I'll see what I can find out. But this is the *last* favor I'm doing for you, *demon*." She turned to leave, shaking her head and muttering under her breath something about a death wish and having to find another demon queen soon, one not as human, frail, and inexperienced as Sadie.

But she couldn't be sure she heard those exact words. They seemed to have been spoken purposefully, but in a way that would make Sadie question the exact meaning of the words. She glared at the angel as she left, a few choice words on the edge of her tongue, but she bit them back for the sake of their so-called alliance, knowing she couldn't afford to make enemies of angels. Evangeline would probably waste no time in reporting back to the others if they were to get into an argument or fight.

The door sealed, with that arrogant angel on the other side, and Sadie let out a breath she didn't realize she had been holding. Damien sighed as well, the tension in his shoulders loosening as they lowered into a more relaxed position.

She smiled at him as he turned to face her. "I'm *your* woman, huh?"

"Well, I mean, you are but I... uh... you know what I mean." He ran his hand through his hair between his horns. "I just got caught up in the moment."

Sadie laughed. "Relax. I'll let that slide just this once. But, just so we're clear, I belong to no one." She winked. "Besides, I'm not an object to own, and I'm not a pet."

She wrapped her arms around him and gave him a kiss. "*However*, the gesture was really sweet. I appreciate that you and your brothers are protective of me."

She pulled away. "Tell me a about your allies. Would any of them join us?"

Damien pursed his eyebrows. "For what? A war against my father?"

"Who else?" she said.

He shook his head. "We may not have time."

"I understand we may not have time to gather a large standing army, but actively recruiting now is a lot better than waiting until you father shows up with his forces and there's only the five of us to face him."

"I will see what I can do, but it will take time," Damien said.

She nodded. Maybe she could get the empusa on her side. They were supposed to be loyal to the demon queen. But the last time she came across them didn't go well. She reasoned that though the first group was against her, loyal to Hecate, that didn't mean *all* of them were. She would ask Hobson about it later.

Despite the possibility that none of those creatures will choose to abandon Hecate, it was still worth a shot. Considering she had her men, staked her claim on her land, and had proven herself queen, how could the empusa refuse?

"What about the empusa?" she asked.

He shook his head. "No. Absolutely not. Do you not remember what happened the last time?"

"Of course, but that was a group, not the entire race of empusa."

He approached her and took her face in his hands, gently cupping her cheeks. "Sadie, they are mindless creatures that were too stubborn to follow direction much less think beyond their own needs. They could very well turn against you in the heart of battle. They are drawn to power, bloodlust, and are simply uncontrollable." He kissed the top of her nose. "I would go crazy if something happened to you. We'll get allies. Just, please, don't try to get *them*."

"Okay, well then tell me about your allies. What should I know about them?"

He removed his hands and they walked through the halls. "Witches and warlocks would be a good addition to any force."

Sadie didn't know much, if anything, about them. But they sounded like a good choice, and she trusted Damien, so she agreed.

"I can take you topside. Introduce you to a witch I think would be a good fit. I trust her, but she's been hesitant to align herself with any demon. Since she's unaligned, and incredibly powerful, she's highly sought after."

"What's her name?"

"Astrid. The most powerful witch that has yet to bond with a demon."

"Why hasn't she bonded with a demon?" she asked.

"She doesn't trust demons. She and I have a steady alliance because we exchange favors every now and again. It also helps that I saved her from my father when he demanded that she join him."

She nodded as she dragged her fingers over the stone walls in the halls of her fortress, each bump and crevice were felt through her entire being. The energy of the place filled her with warmth, pulsing in rhythm with her heartbeats. She sighed.

"Do you think she will work with us?"

"You'll have to prove yourself to her to get her help, but if she agrees to fight with us, we will be that much closer to defeating my father."

"What do you think she will require of me in order to prove myself? Why should I have to?" The thought instantly frustrated her. If anything, it should be Astrid proving herself to Sadie, not the other way around.

"Relax, you only have to show her you can be trusted. If anyone can get Astrid on their team, I have the utmost confidence it is you."

She seemed like an asset they needed, if she was as powerful as Damien claimed. And because she had no reason to doubt him, she figured it was worth a shot.

Prove herself trustworthy? Hadn't she wanted the same of her men?

Finally, she nodded and turned down an adjacent hall that led to one of her gardens. She needed to think. When she didn't hear footsteps following, she stopped and turned. Damien stood in the middle of the hall with his hands in his pants pockets, watching her expectantly.

She smiled. "Well, are you coming?"

He smiled back and followed.

CHAPTER FOUR

DAMIEN

*A*s they arrived at the gardens, Hobson was tending to some of the hedges. He hummed to himself as he worked, and Damien wondered if the gargoyle truly enjoyed what he did. A life of servitude.

Sadie had her arm in the crook of Damen's elbow. She reached out and gently brushed a petal of a bright orange flower with her fingers. She smiled, and he could see the gears turning in her head.

"What are you thinking about?" he asked. What he would give to have Steele's ability to enter her mind.

"The differences between witches and warlocks. Since coming here, I've learned that stories and myths from the topside got a lot of things wrong about angels and demons. What do I need to know about witches and warlocks?"

"I can try to explain that to you, if you would like."

He may not have been able to read her mind, but at least he could help put it at ease.

She smiled, setting her dark eyes on him, lighting his blood on fire and quickening his pulse. "I would love that."

He nodded and led her to a spot in a small clearing. After making sure she was settled, he stood off to the side and said, "First, only women are witches."

"Oh, if you don't mind," Hobson said as he approached the small clearing, "I can illuminate on this topic as you explain."

Damien nodded. "Very well."

Hobson conjured a sphere of magic, clear with the luminescence of light in the way that a bubble would shine in the sun.

"Witches are humans who get their powers from demons," Damien said.

An image of a human woman standing next to a demon appeared in the bubble. Sadie smiled as she glanced at him then back to the image. Damien wanted to ask about that, but then he quickly realized he was a demon and she was human. That must've been what she thought they looked like standing next to each other.

"On the whole," he said, "witches are corrupted souls who have devoted their lives as well as their deaths to a demon of the underworld. That is referred to as bonding."

The image shifted, and a silver-blue line threaded from the witch to the demon. The outline of the demon turned brighter while the outline of the witch darkened, and shadowy vapor seemed to waft from her form.

"Once the witch dies, her soul is absorbed by the demon…" Damien nodded to the image.

The witch turned into smoke then blended in with the shape of the demon. Damien saw the pained look on Sadie's face. She tried to hide it, but he sensed her discomfort.

"… giving him more strength and power, taking all of the gifts the witch obtained in life."

The demon demonstrated lightning, growing stone from the ground, and calling forth heavy winds from a silhouetted wood, uprooting trees and leaving chaos in his wake.

Curiosity seeped from Sadie, her expression was ripe with it. He wondered, what about that fact he just said caused her to be curious.

"This is what makes a witch a sought-after prize that demons will do anything to empower and train. However, very few souls are kept on-hand as envoys, forced to live an afterlife of servitude benefiting the demon."

"Like Astrid?" she asked.

"Yes. Like Astrid," Damien said.

The shadowy smoke of the witch's corrupted soul

left the demon, taking a form akin to a wraith. The demon pointed in a direction, the wraith turned and floated away toward its master's bidding.

Damien shifted to face Sadie, sensing her confusion. "Any questions?"

"A few, actually." She nibbled on her lower lip.

Damien couldn't stop staring when she did that. He wanted to press those lips into his and show her what it really meant to nibble. He just wouldn't stop at her lips. He cleared his throat and blinked that thought away. "Such as?"

"Why would a witch commit herself to a demon and risk everlasting peace?"

"Good question. What else?" he asked.

"You didn't even answer the first," she said, giving him a pointed look.

"Some don't commit themselves, Your Highness," Hobson said. "Such unfortunate souls."

"Why?" she asked. "I mean, why are they unfortunate souls for not bonding with a demon?"

Damien answered, "Some witches are...I guess you'd say, *good*, and want to remain uncorrupted. However, they are largely slaughtered because they are seen as weak-minded, even though they are stronger and can fight longer with their magic."

Hobson added, "In many ways, Your Majesty, witches are forced into their bonding to suit a specific purpose. If a witch chooses not to bond, she is essentially seen as a threat. Though many families have carried the belief that an unbonded witch is lesser and weaker, she is potentially much stronger than those who have bonded."

Sadie shook her head. "I'm getting lost."

"Perhaps I can clear things up a bit," Damien said. "The strength of a witch's magical ability is determined mainly by her heritage. If she's in a family that has served demons for eons, she'll be far more powerful than newer families, because magical ability is passed on through generations and becomes stronger with every new one."

"I'm following," she said, nodding.

He continued, "This tends to lead to a lot of classism within the ranks of witches. However, some demons can give witches more magic than others, depending on if that witch can handle it and if the demon has the power to give."

Hobson said, "A witch can choose not to serve a demon, even if her family does, but the consequence is that many of them are killed. They believe she can only realize her true strength if she serves a demon."

Sadie narrowed her eyes as that crease between her eyebrows formed. Damien knew she was making connections and the gears were turning in her head. She turned her gaze on him, and he wanted to gulp, lock his knees to keep them from buckling under the weight of her stare and stop himself from just taking her right then and there.

This woman.

Only she could make him weak in the knees, cradle him in desire, and cause him to quake under her gaze.

He forced back a growl.

"And how many witches have you bonded with?" she asked, chewing that lip again.

"None," he said, flatly.

She cocked her head to the side. Her dark hair cascaded over her shoulder, baring her delicious neck, ripe for the kissing, nibbling, and blood rushing touches that would make her melt in his arms.

"Why not?" she asked.

"Magic can be given in many ways, though it's often transmitted and granted sexually. Doing it this way builds a connection to their demon, too, which can *never* be broken."

"Does that sort of commitment bother you? A Big, bad demon, like yourself?"

She was toying with him now, and he knew it. That only made him want her more.

He had to be next to her. Smell her. Touch her. He took a seat on the grass next to her. "I only want to be bonded with you, Sadie. No one else, witch or no."

"How do you know I'm not a witch? I've seemed to have caught you under a rather dangerous spell." She leaned in closer to him, the tip of her nose brushed his chin and his pants grew even tighter.

"You have certainly enchanted me," he said.

She kissed him, and he cupped her cheek. Hobson cleared his throat. "If you are done, I have more hedges that need trimmed."

Damn. I forgot he was there. "Yes, I'm finished."

Sadie sat up straight. "No, you're not. You haven't told me about warlocks."

"Right. We still don't need Hobson's demonstrations." He looked to the butler. "You are free to go."

Hobson nodded and went about his way.

Settling in closer to Sadie, Damien said. "Warlocks are the male counterparts of witches, but they process magic in a different way. They can only access power through the use of infused weapons which are mostly minor and short range. They are limited and less desired but can still bring an enemy to his knees if they are in large enough numbers."

That spot in Sadie's forehead appeared again, and her eyes became distant. Any second now, she would chew her lip, and Damien wasn't sure he could restrain himself.

"I want to see them for myself," she said. "Will you take me?"

He struggled to hide the disappointment he felt when she skipped over his favorite part. He smiled at her, kissed her forehead and said, "I will personally see to it that you are able to meet a few of them. They can easily pull up portals to the underworld and be here when I call. It would be even better if you could get the demons that control them on your side as well."

Sadie smiled and kissed him. She seemed to bubble over in excitement, which made Damien chuckle.

The rest of the evening was spent answering questions and spending time with his woman.

~

SADIE

*J*ust before her bath, Sadie made her way to her weapons room and took stock of everything. If she were to get warlocks on her force, she would need suitable weapons for them.

She processed the information Damien shared with her, and she wondered what it would be like to meet one in person, and if she had unwittingly met one before. She didn't want to rely on preconceived notions or Hollywood's depictions, but she also didn't know what to expect.

Especially with the little note about demons having to have sex with a witch to bond with her. She didn't like the idea of any of her men having bonding, sexual rites with any woman.

Down girl. Taking a calming breath, she made her way to her small room. She trusted her men and believed Damien when he said he hadn't bonded with anyone. Her initial reaction was silly when she considered the reality of it all.

Entering the small room, her eyes took in her battle dress that hung neatly on its mannequin, all cleaned up and repaired from the last battle she had worn it in. Her sword hummed to her the second she drew nearer. She loved that sword.

Maybe it was initially used by a warlock? Hecate, she had learned, was known for being ruthless and taking a sword that had the incredible power hers did, certainly seemed like a thing that would happen.

Then again, maybe that's how the previous queen acquired all of her weapons. By taking them.

Either way, they were hers now.

Satisfied by the stock of weapons, she left the weapons room and headed straight for her bath. The hot water would help relax her, and she could further reflect on her newfound information.

CHAPTER FIVE

SADIE

"*Halt!*" Sadie called out to Pyra, her pet dragon. She trained in one of her courtyards with the creature to practice commands.

Pyra instantly responded, digging her claws into the earth, kicking up clouds of dust behind her. She bent her neck to look back at Sadie and gave a little growling purr which made a laugh bubble out of her chest.

"Good girl. Now, to me."

The dragon spun, wings catching the light and glinting in reds, oranges, and yellows, and rushed to Sadie's side and nuzzled her hand. Her eyes took in Sadie's and she instantly felt that fun, close, and loving energy that made them so connected. Sadie responded with a good scratch to the top of her head.

Next, Sadie conjured up some smoke walls, reinforcing them with extra strength and setting several of them throughout the courtyard in a makeshift obstacle course. As she did so, she considered revisiting Hecate to further glean information from the dead queen about why she's so feared and hated... maybe even gain some insight into how she could handle her latest threat.

"Seek," she said.

Pyra took off, climbing over walls, crawling around them, and knocking some over, making them dissipate into nothing before colliding with the ground.

Then she recalled what happened the last time she went to get information from Hecate and wondered if they had just started off on the wrong foot. Perhaps, if she put her foot down and told Hecate that she was dead and had had her time, and now it was her turn to deal with being the demon queen, the ghost would finally back off and accept her fate.

But she didn't want to further fuel whatever hate the dead queen seemed to harbor for her either. If siphoning a part of her soul was a sign of hate to begin with.

She was still new to this world and the rules that came with it.

Her men would likely be displeased if she tried to go in alone again.

Maybe if she took all four of them, that would save

her the headache of hearing about it later? They could help ward off another attack. And if Hecate attacked, that would prove to Sadie that her and the ghost were at odds. She would then have to figure out how to best handle the previous queen.

Either way, she needed answers.

At some point during Sadie's reflection, Pyra had grown bored of the walls and started to chase some small insect through the courtyard. Waving a hand, Sadie dismissed the remaining walls and wondered if the dragon would play fetch.

Focusing on her hand, she felt the tug of warmth from her amulet, forming a ball of purple light, making it pliable and solid. The ball sparked as it grew into an orb of bright yellow light.

Satisfied by her creation, Sadie reared her hand back and threw the ball, catapulting it to the far corner of the courtyard.

Pyra immediately ran after it. Sadie laughed.

Well, what do you know? I have a dragon that plays fetch. How fun!

Sadie threw the ball up into the air and watched as Pyra wiggled her butt, eyes on the ball, then pushed off with her back legs into the air. She flapped her wings, soaring higher, aiming for the ball. Catching it in her mouth, she spiraled downward, landing on the grass.

That gave Sadie a thought.

Pyra's strength was in the air. She could use that in a battle to launch devastating fireballs toward the ground and her enemies. She could also train her dragon to evade counter attacks.

Using her mental connection with her pet, Sadie told the dragon to fly and avoid getting hit. The dragon cocked her head to the side and made a grunt. Sadie giggled.

"Trust me," she said before conjuring balls of smoke and shadow.

Pyra launched into the air as she tossed the balls up.

Sadie sent commands in intervals... bank left, swerve right, dive. She studied the way her dragon moved and knew she could hone her pet's skills for use if need be.

Of course, Pyra would need armor.

She sent the ball of light up into the air in another direction then tossed balls of smoke and shadow for the dragon to avoid in its pursuit of the prize, making sure to use her mental connection with her pet to help avoid injury.

Pyra obeyed. Not only that, but it was fun, and the dragon seemed to enjoy herself as well.

Now, she finally had a fun past-time to help relieve stress.

Between throws of the ball for her dragon, Sadie practiced with conjuring the vines. She made little arches with them, adding in walls of smoke to make it even more engaging for Pyra.

Her thoughts eventually wandered back to the queen, and she questioned why Hecate was still even here if she's dead. What could she possibly want to stick around for? Wasn't there some sort of ghostly, demonic paradise waiting for her? A Valhalla for demon queens?

She may not have had the answers to those questions, but there was certainly one who might. Hobson. She would just avoid directly addressing the Hecate topic.

Sadie reached out to the fortress and summoned him.

Moments later, he cleared his throat. "You summoned me, Your Majesty?"

She turned and faced the butler. "Yes, is there an afterlife?"

Hobson stared blankly at her and seemed to wait for a follow-up question. He had remained quiet for so long, she wondered if he had turned into a statue.

He rapidly blinked and said, "For what purpose is your question?"

She shrugged. "Curiosity."

"Is that all?" he asked, a stony eyebrow lifted as his eyes slightly narrowed.

He apparently didn't believe curiosity was the only reason for asking. She had to think of a way to quickly get some answers without directly referencing the dead queen haunting the south wing.

She nodded. "Mmm-hmm!"

"I'm not aware of such a thing existing. When we die, we are typically absorbed by whatever killed us, or we become nothing."

Unless you're Hecate, apparently. She nodded as she bit her lip. There had to be more of a reason why that woman's ghost was stuck in her fortress. Maybe she was trapped here somehow. Or maybe there were more sinister things at work than just a malevolent ghost meandering the halls of the fortress. Sadie just couldn't guess as to what.

"Is there anything else?" Hobson asked with his arms behind him.

"What about the empusa?" Sadie wondered how the creatures could still be so loyal to a woman that shouldn't even exist if Hobson's theory was correct.

"What about them?" he asked, creases of worry continued to wrinkle his brow.

"Are all of them loyal to Hecate?" she asked.

Hobson's shoulders relaxed as he let out a heavy breath. Sadie wanted to ask what he thought she was going to ask, but he beat her to the punch and said, "Most of them are. However, I do believe there are a few groups who aren't."

"I wonder if there is a way to find out where they

are?" Sadie asked, staring off at a single blade of grass poking through a stone of a walkway.

"If I may, Your Highness," Hobson said, "empusa would definitely not fit well within your rule. Remember that they are mindless creatures. I worry they would turn on you sooner than follow you."

Sadie nodded. "Thank you. I'll take that under advisement. You may go."

"Very well." He nodded and left.

Meanwhile, Sadie needed a plan to get more allies. She also needed answers. And she couldn't get them if she stood around playing with Pyra all day.

She called to her dragon, who came obediently. After giving her a loving pet on the head and neck, she guided Pyra back to her stable and headed for one of the places she was sure would give her answers.

The south wing.

CHAPTER SIX

MORDECAI

*M*ordecai stood hidden within the shadows. He loved the way it felt to be unseen, the weightlessness of floating and the quick travel, since he could slip through cracks and avoid the whole business of walking. Not that he was lazy, but the mere feeling of being shadow was addicting, and he used his ability any chance he got.

Footsteps echoed toward him, pulling his attention to Sadie. She had that determined look in her eyes, which made Mordecai wonder what she was up to. He smiled as she chewed on her lip, walking with extreme purpose down the hall.

She's so damned adorable. How the hell can a woman be both adorable and badass at the same time?

He would do anything for her. Spend eternity with her. He had never known love until her or realized just how incredibly lonely he was. He felt he had a purpose now. She had become the center of his universe, and that also meant if she was up to something, he needed to know what. Besides, it would be fun to just see how long he could get away with it.

Still hidden, he followed Sadie down the halls of the fortress leading to the foyer and throne room. Keeping his distance, clothed with stealth, he watched as she stopped and cocked her head to the side.

She turned and faced him. "Why are you sneaking around and following me?"

Her lips were set in a firm line, but those eyes. Ah, yes. Those eyes were soft and held a light in them. That told him she really wasn't mad at him. Just frustrated. He smiled again, knowing he was getting a rise out of her. It thrilled him, and he loved being able to calm the storm he caused within her.

She focused on his smile, and the tension in her shoulders relaxed a little. She grinned and shook her head.

"What are you up to?" he asked her, narrowing his eyes on her, keeping his debonair, suave tone even. Just the way she liked it.

"I wanted to go to the south wing to speak with Hecate."

Something in him shifted at the mention of the previous demon queen's name. He knew full and well what happened the last time she visited the queen. If he remembered correctly, he and his brothers all forbade her from going there again.

Not gonna happen.

Her eyes focused on his, and he knew they had turned red with the level of anger and protection that had risen within him. "No."

It came out firm. No room to argue here.

She scoffed, rolling her eyes and propping a hand on her sumptuous hip. Damn that woman.

"I was going to get you and your brothers. We were all going to go."

Mordecai wasn't having any of it though. The risk was too great. He shook his head again and stepped closer to her. "No."

Again, firm.

Her eyes darkened, and she stood a bit straighter. She was so cute when she was angry.

"Fine. I'll just go by myself. I need answers only she can give me."

He gripped her hips and pulled her closer, refusing to let go.

She sighed. "Look," her voice had softened, "I appreciate your protectiveness, but I won't get anywhere as queen if I don't have information on what it means to be queen, who her enemies were and why, and what I can do to stop a war. I also want to know if any of her allies are still around. I can't do that without talking to her. I understand the dangers, which was why I mentioned having you and your brothers with me."

"I don't like it," he said. "Hecate wasn't exactly known for being the giving kind, especially with information."

She pulled away from him and started for the south wing.

He growled and followed her, determined to talk some sense into her.

Stubbornness was just one of the many frustrating qualities Sadie had. A quality he loved about her. But he would be damned if he just let her walk right in front of that ghost, much less without him.

As they walked, he managed to remain a few steps behind. "You don't seem to fully grasp just how close to death you were during your last little visit, do you?"

She didn't respond.

He picked up his pace and gripped her arm, forcing her to turn around. She leveled her gaze on him. Anger lit up her eyes. "I can't let you go through with this, Sadie."

The thought of his woman falling prey to a woman so vile and wretched, even in spectral form, caused his nerves to shiver and his heart didn't seem to want to find a happy, even rhythm.

No. He wouldn't let her go through with it. Damn the consequences.

"Let go of me, now!" She tried to wrench her arm

from his grasp, but it was no use. He held on, refusing to let her throw herself to the proverbial wolves... and Hecate was supreme alpha bitch.

"You are no good to anyone dead. Until we can figure out a way to protect you from her, me and my brothers will do whatever it takes to keep you safe and away from harm." To further prove his point, he pushed her back against the stone wall. Her reaction didn't escape his notice. Her eyes narrowed, and her cheeks took on a rosy tint. She slightly melted against him.

He rubbed the blush in her cheeks and asked in a dark, husky voice, "If it is so important to you to get the information you seek, tell me what it is you want to know, and I'll go in there and ask. You stay out here, safe."

Searching her eyes, he saw the need within her growing. He smiled, devilish and promising. "Or, I could just take what I want from you right here and now."

He pushed up against her even farther and kissed her neck.

Of course, Sadie was strong enough to handle herself. Mordecai of all people knew that very well. He had trained with her when they first met, and he saw firsthand what she could do. She was impressive, controlled, focused. She even spoke with the finesse of a true leader, commanding the attention of those under her rule.

But he could never let her go through with it. He wanted to be in control. He wanted to be protective. And damnit, she was his woman. He wasn't going to allow his woman to be in danger.

Not ever.

Sadie laughed. His beard must have tickled the inside of her neck. She pushed him away. "Nice try."

"Come on, Sadie." He tried to convince her one, last time. "Please understand this doesn't need to happen right now. Our main focus needs to be on Zagan. The ghost can't help with that. She's dead and trapped in the south wing. I refuse to budge on this. Give me that, at least this once."

She sighed, giving in. "Fine. But—"

He rushed her, scooping her into his arms, and kissed her deeply. The taste of her mouth was sweet, and he wanted more of that warm, tingling sensation that coursed through his body. He wanted her to give into him completely. And he could tell she got close to that as she pressed farther into him, moving her mouth with his.

This was it.

He was finally about to seal the deal when she pushed him away again, chuckling.

"I'll avoid the queen. But something needs to be done about her soon if she's truly a threat to me. I can't have an enemy in my fortress. Even an undead one."

He groaned as the need in him ached, but he agreed, and pulled away, allowing her to stand on her own. "Absolutely, Captain."

This was a draw. A stalemate. He won the argument this time, though she won in resisting him.

He will have her, and soon. Or he just may go fucking crazy.

A sensation prickled through him. Narrowing his eyes, he focused on that sensation and shifted into shadow.

Sadie had sensed the change as well.

She followed him in the direction of the power that put him on edge.

They arrived at the front door to the fortress, and he floated through the shadows to get to the gates.

In the distance, his father approached with only ten to twelve men at his side.

What are you playing at, father?

Zagan loved to show his force before pleasantries. It was a way to keep the masses weak and feeble toward him. Though, he preferred to avoid the whole ordeal of pleasantries if he could help it. He loved his torture. It was like a drug to him. But he didn't have an army backing him that Mordecai could see or sense. This felt like a trap. Perhaps his father was deluded enough to think Sadie would take his little warning to heart.

Did they have a surprise for *him*.

There was something more to the arrival of his father, though. Mordecai sensed as much. Be it trap or otherwise.

His brothers soon joined him. He could feel the tension among them at the arrival of their father. Sadie followed shortly after with her own little show of force in her favorite battle dress and Pyra walking beside her. If looks could kill, Sadie had this visit on lock.

He smiled.

Let the action begin.

CHAPTER SEVEN

SADIE

*Z*agan stood outside of Sadie's gate. And he had a smaller group with him than he did the first time he arrived. At least he didn't sit atop a dragon he controlled. He actually walked. Perhaps he thought that would make a difference to Sadie, but it didn't. Her mind was made up. And Zagan had no right to tell her otherwise.

Pyra growled from beside Sadie. She petted the dragon and tried to soothe her as much as possible. Everyone was on edge with the appearance of the demon king.

"You still have yet to learn when to allow someone who is visiting you through your gates," he said.

Sadie narrowed her eyes on him and didn't let him through. The fact he brought what she assumed to be guards unsettled her. He was supposed to be a danger and always backed by an army, so what was he doing with just a handful of demons at his side. It didn't make sense, and the lack of army unsettled her. She knew there was more to the visit than what met her eyes, and she tuned into her connection with the fortress.

If anyone else was on her land, she didn't feel them. Or Zagan had them outside her boundaries.

Maybe he figured she would take his threat to heart and pick him over his sons? Sadie nearly snorted. She held it in and forced back the urge to roll her eyes instead. The visit would still take a considerable amount of tact.

"I demand the respect I deserve by allowing me within your walls to discuss matters like civilized rulers."

She stood firm, head held high. "No. You'll be allowed through that gate once I say so. Not a moment before. And by the looks of it, you're not off to a great start."

Her men shifted their weight between their feet on either side of her, watching the threat expectantly, like they were itching for a taste of battle.

"I am king!" he shouted, spittle spraying from his mouth.

"Not my king. And certainly not over my land," Sadie said.

He laughed. "I admire your tact. Your ability to

stand your ground and stick to your guns." He pointed a finger at her. "Very well. Let's move on to the reason for my visit."

She rolled her eyes. "I know why you are here, Zagan."

He paused and slowly nodded. "And?"

"I've made my decision on who I would choose to be my ally. I regret to inform Your Majesty, you didn't make the cut." She held her head high, ready for the repercussions of her next words. Ready for war. "But your sons did. I have chosen all of them."

Zagan turned rigid, nearly shaking with rage that poured off him like thick fog. "I warned you, did I not, that choosing any of my sons would be considered an act of war."

"Yes, you did. However, I'm perfectly capable of making decisions of my own, without the threat of death and violence."

He continued as if Sadie hadn't spoken. "Yet, instead of choosing just me, you chose not only one of my sons, but all of four?" He shook his head and made a ticking sound. "Now that won't do at all."

"Works perfectly fine from my perspective," Sadie said, still standing her ground, refusing to back down.

"That's too much power for you. Power that threatens my seat on the throne. The very throne that my sons have been trying to kill me to claim. Did you know that? Oh, yes. It's true! You are a powerplay. A puppet. And I just won't stand to see my seat claimed by the likes of you or my sons."

He turned to leave and signaled to the distance, shooting a bolt of fire into the air like a flare. As it rose higher toward the ceiling of the underworld, it grew bigger, whiter, hotter.

A dull roar echoed toward Sadie and her men.

This was it. The fight he had promised.

The roar grew louder as an even bigger army grew from tiny silhouettes to larger forms. Goblins, other demons, creatures she could only guess at, and smoky forms that held little shape but swerved toward them, travelled wickedly fast. They seemed to have enhanced momentum from the witches that Zagan surely had. They moved at such an ungodly speed.

Sadie hadn't sensed them. Only the smaller army Zagan had brought with him. He must have known she could tell when someone stepped onto her land and wanted to use the larger force to overthrow her the moment she turned him down. He accounted for that possibility. And with the sheer numbers heading for them, Sadie worried he would succeed.

She shifted her gaze to Zagan, who stared from over his shoulder at her with a devious grin.

"Pyra," she said, and climbed on top of her. She wouldn't let Zagan get away. Not if she could help it. "Fly!"

The dragon pushed off with its strong hind legs and soared into the air.

Zagan faced her, eyes narrowed on her and that grin replaced by a deep frown. He lifted a hand.

A large gust of wind blew into her and the dragon. The force was strong enough to send Pyra spiraling backward. Sadie lost her grip on her pet and fell, crashing hard to the ground with a heavy thump. Pain ricocheted through her arm, back and shoulders. Sharp throbs shot up her leg when her ankle landed at an odd angle. Her hands burned from the sting of tiny rocks that had embedded into her palms.

Still, she stood, biting against the pain that coursed through her. Quickly, she searched for Pyra, finding her not far from where Sadie stood. She seemed a little jarred, but otherwise unharmed. She sighed with relief and leveled her gaze on the demon king and conjured up a bow and arrow made of smoke.

Rage burned within Zagan's eyes. "Get to my sons. Slaughter them or be slaughtered yourself."

They charged the gate. The princes met them there.

Sadie shot a smoke arrow toward the demon king. He waved it away with a flick of his wrist then sent another gust of wind into her. "Let me in! I'm far more powerful than you. Open your gates and the fight will end. Or, continue your obstinate defiance and watch your army, my sons, and your fortress fall brick by brick, limb by limb."

"Never!" She quickly conjured a smoke shield to block the next gust to come after her.

Pyra flew past her, blowing fire at the soldiers hacking at the gate to enter Sadie's fortress. The dragon let out a loud, painful howl and fell to the ground.

"No!" Sadie rushed to her pet, taking out a few skeletons trying to surround the poor creature with her fire magic.

Zagan called to her. "Demon Queen, reconsider, and this will all end."

Fat chance.

After making sure Pyra wasn't gravely injured, she faced the demon king again. "I will never surrender to you!"

He moved quickly, sending a blast of fire, engulfing the gates of the fortress in blue flames.

Now, Sadie was pissed. She had enough of demons using fire to destroy her home. She lost her apartment that way, and she refused to let her fortress fall to the likes of an egomaniac like Zagan. His temper tantrum would end before the gate fell. Come hell or high water. All because she said no.

Boo fucking hoo. Get over it.

She shot some shadow arrows at him. One landed in his shoulder. It didn't do much damage, except prevent him from being able to shoot more fire at her gate.

He smiled at her. And as if he knew what she thought, he proved her wrong by adding more blasts of blue flames to the gate.

The metal screeched and whined.

Sadie rushed forward, stopping just outside of the heat of the flames consuming her gate. She conjured metal vines from the ground in hopes of reinforcing the gates. But they burnt to a crisp before they could do much good.

Since that didn't work, she aimed them toward Zagan. He shrugged them off effortlessly, never wavering from his casting.

Frustrated, she threw everything she could think of at him. Fireballs, vines, shadow arrows, smoke walls. Nothing fazed him.

Why won't you just die! Zagan came prepared. He seemed to know when she was going to attack and with what, and that angered her even more. She wanted him gone, the fight to be over, and be done with him for good. But she just couldn't land a good enough hit to him. And his forces were making short work of the gate, seeping through in small clusters, going after her and her men.

If Sadie was going to succeed in this battle, she needed to be quicker, out-smart him. And that was where the problem lay.

Creatures started to break through the gates. Goblins, skeletons, and demons alike. The wraiths shot lightning toward the princes. Mordecai, of course, had shifted into shadow. Kaiser shot fire at the creatures, and Steele dodged each bolt. Damien used Lightbane to somehow absorb the bolts.

Sadie sighed in relief.

What she thought was a goblin dashed toward her, slashing her leg with its long, talon-like nails. No, this wasn't a goblin. This was something else entirely. A hybrid, a horrific creature with pale skin and solid black eyes and sharp teeth that protruded from its mouth. She summoned her smoke sword and fire shield. She used the shield to burn the skin of the creature, filling her nose with powerful, vomit-inducing stench that clung to the back of her throat.

Dizziness swam through her and she struggled to stay on her feet. She slashed with her sword, nearly blind from the tears that welled up in her eyes from the aroma of the creature's blood. The blade sank into the creature's skin like a hot knife through butter. She squeezed her eyes shut in an effort to clear the sting and tears from her eyes then went for the next creature. She continued using the vines to ensnare oncoming hordes of Zagan's army.

Sadie refused to let this be her last fight.

CHAPTER EIGHT

SADIE

*S*adie's bruises darkened, and her arms and back throbbed with pain. She was tired and covered from head to toe in the result of her carnage. She wasn't sure where the blood of the creatures she killed ended and hers began. But the fight wasn't over yet. She would worry about tending to wounds and getting cleaned up soon enough.

Zagan continued to send more of his troops to the gate. Sadie and her men, along with Pyra, fought the best they could to keep the gate from completely collapsing. Her men seemed worse for the wear, but she couldn't assess the extent of their injuries to be sure. Each time she dismantled a skeleton, took out a demon, goblin, or one of those other scarier creatures, another one took its place.

This wasn't working. She needed to think of something to get the upper hand on the fight and fast.

Zagan stood just outside of Sadie's reach, his smug expression showing that he was rather pleased with himself for turning the tide in his favor.

Sadie was done with this. Tapping into the power in her amulet, she pulled from the energy what she could and screamed as she held her hands out in front of her, sending bright steams of fire from her to the advancing soldiers and then toward Zagan.

The earth beneath her feet and the stalagmites on the ceiling shook. Some fell off, crushing some of Zagan's forces.

But before she spent too much time processing what she had just done, as it was new and different, she refocused herself as another one of the demon king's soldiers came after her. She stood, prepared to fight with her shadow sword and flaming shield as a loud roar came from behind, growing in force and intensity the closer the sound drew.

She peeked over her shoulder to find her ifrits, in all their blazing fiery-orange glory, charging the fortress grounds toward the gates, weapons held high and ready for battle.

She hoped that they would be enough to even the odds if not tip the war in her favor.

Facing her opponent, she dispatched him and shouted at Zagan. "Enough of this, coward! Face me and fight me like a king, instead of hiding behind your army."

Zagan narrowed his eyes on her. "You chose this by forcing my hand. I cannot stand by as my sons plot to overthrow me with you by their side. I warned you. You disregarded that. This is your chosen fate."

Sadie wasn't taking excuses. Especially his excuses. She used her mental connection with Pyra and urged her pet dragon to flank Zagan.

One way or another, Sadie was ending this fight before any lives were lost on her side.

Pyra landed behind Zagan, inching up behind him. He turned and faced the dragon, palms igniting in purple-blue light.

Oh no you don't.

Sadie used her fire shield to launch a fire missile at his back. Zagan's magic faltered. The glow dissipated. He turned to face her again, anger forcing his eyes to turn red and glow with fury.

She stepped toward him with determined purpose, her eyes never wavering from him. At the same point, Pyra urged him closer to her. Once she was within the appropriate distance to run him through with her sword, she conjured the vines, commanding them to wrap around Zagan's ankles. She struggled to get them around his torso and arms as he fought against her, maintaining his foothold and not falling like she hoped he would.

She was close now. Fate was on her side. Zagan's forces were being slaughtered one-by-one, lowering his numbers, and she just had to get close enough to him to land the final blow.

Zagan looked around as he struggled to break the vines around his ankles. Finally, they snapped, and he said, "Enough!"

His voice echoed over the battlefield and his soldiers stopped advancing.

He settled his gaze on her and breathed heavily. "This isn't the last of me. I will return. And when I do, you will join me. I'll take everything from you until you do." He pointed at her. "I'll have you. One way or another. You started this war. You'll do well to remember that when you lose to me."

"Good luck with that." Her words were thick with sarcasm and she let her shield and sword disappear. "Now, leave."

"Retreat. To me!" he shouted and turned on his heels to return home.

They won. But just barely.

Though they managed to work together and take out a great number of Zagan's forces, they didn't escape unscathed. Steele was hurt. Bad. He clutched his side and hobbled toward Sadie. Blood oozed from around his fingers. Damien and Kaiser ran to his side and wrapped an arm around him just as his knees gave out from under him. Mordecai joined Sadie, face sullen and worn.

Steele was pale. And Sadie feared the worst.

As they worked to keep their brother on his feet, Sadie ran to him, worry pulsing through her as she took in more of the injuries Steele endured. She was worried for her prince, and as she arrived, he faintly smiled.

"Don't worry about me, love. You should see the other guy." He chuckled, but it was weak and lacking the luster his carefree attitude normally held.

Sadie smiled, just the same, appreciating that even as close to death as he was, he still maintained his humor despite the pain he must have felt. "Don't worry. You can tell me all about it when you are better."

She summoned Hobson.

"Yes—oh, dear." Hobson's eyebrows knitted together, and his lips pulled down at the corners as he took in Steele's condition. He shook his head. "Majesty, the infirmary has special tinctures to aid in his healing. I'll hurry after those. Meanwhile, use your magic to cauterize the wounds. I'm sure one of the princes will help you if need be."

"Please hurry, Hobson," Sadie said.

Hobson nodded then and rushed off.

Sadie pointed to the ground. "Lay him down so I can seal his wounds."

Damien and Kaiser nodded and did so as gently as possible. Steele winced, otherwise Sadie knew he tried to hide the pain he felt. Mordecai stood back, watching with wide eyes and a deep frown.

"Don't worry. He'll be okay."

He muttered something under his breath about checking the perimeters of the boundary and walked off. Sadie felt for him, but in order to make good on her promise that Steele would be okay, she needed to seal his wounds.

Sadie quickly knelt next to Steele and peeled back the layers of his armor and under shirt to find a sizeable gash in his side. She tried not to let the seriousness of the wound keep her from her task and summoned the magic from her amulet.

Her hands warmed and started to glow with soft, yellowish red light. She hovered her hands over the wound and said, "Hold him."

Kaiser and Damien each held an arm and pressed on Steele's shoulders as she forced the fire magic from her hands into the large wound.

Steele hissed and grunted as the wound became sealed, and the bleeding stopped. Steele then passed out.

A pinch formed in Sadie's brow as she realized it wasn't just an ordinary weapon that caused his wound and wondered if Hobson noticed the same.

First things first. She needed to get Steele to his bed.

She called for Pyra, who grunted in response. Together, Damien and Kaiser gently lifted Steele to her back. They escorted the dragon to Steele's room and they laid him on top of the bed. Hobson was already there, mixing tinctures and concoctions together to form a paste. Once he was done, he ripped the remains of Steele's armor from him and let the air fill the wound before applying ample amounts of the paste to it.

Once he was done, he stood back and sighed. "I'm afraid the rest is up to him."

Sadie placed a hand on his shoulder. "Thank you for your help."

He seemed like he still wasn't used to her politeness as he stammered a "you're welcome" and excused himself from the room.

Damien said, "I'll take first watch."

"No," Sadie said. "I will. You each have your own wounds to tend to."

Kaiser said, "And you don't?"

"Yes," she said. "But he's here because of me."

"No, he's not, Sadie," Damien said. "He's here because of our father."

Sadie bit back the tears that formed in her eyes and nodded. She knew that was true, but that didn't erase the guilt she felt. "Give me this. Please." She settled her gaze on Damien and then Kaiser.

They all stood in silence for a moment. The men likely debated another rebuttal. But she stood firm and refused to leave, taking a seat on the bed to prove her point. She covered Steele's hand with hers and watched as he slept. His eyelids were a deep purple, and his skin was too pale. The sheen from his golden skin was missing, and she wanted so desperately for him to be better right then and there.

The door silently sealed.

Sadie looked to where Damien and Kaiser had been standing and found that they had obeyed her wish by letting her have this moment with their brother.

She nodded to herself and laid down next to him, gently running her fingers over the curves and angles of his chest, loving on him and wishing him well.

Though she was grateful to have him there, she hated how hurt he was. She knew there was nothing more she could do besides wait and hope he woke up soon.

After a while of his breathing returning to a normal pace and the muscles in his body relaxing, she left for the war room. She needed a plan for the next time Zagan showed up ready for war, and she needed it now.

SADIE

*A*s she entered the war room, Damien, Kaiser, and Mordecai were discussing their surprise at their father's surge in power.

"I just don't understand it," Kaiser said. "He was stronger than before."

"And that's the problem," Mordecai said.

"Perhaps he gained another witch and consumed her soul?" Damien said.

Mordecai shook his head. "No, he would've had to have dispatched dozens of them just to get a fraction of that power. He's callous, but not stupid. That would've cut his numbers significantly and made it to where no other witches or warlocks would join him."

"There has to be a reason for it," Damien said and seemed to retreat into his own thoughts.

Sadie said, "Whatever the reason is, we need to find out how and prepare for the next time."

Kaiser snorted. "He probably realized that his normal approach of force and demand wasn't going to work on you and will likely try to get you under his control in a different way."

"And that's the trick, isn't it?" Mordecai asked. "Father has never been the one to change his approach. So, why now?"

"Whatever the reason," Sadie said, "I promise I will do whatever it takes to protect you and my home. I refuse to be forced under his thumb."

"How is he?" Mordecai asked. When Sadie looked at him with an expression of confusion, he added, "My brother. How is he?"

"Sleeping. Peacefully." She sighed and slid into the chair surrounding the war table.

Her men started discussing action plans again while Sadie slipped into her thoughts. She processed the information that even Zagan's sons had no idea what their father was up to. He changed his tactic, and that meant Sadie needed to be on her toes with preparations for the next little visit.

Whatever Zagan was up to, she had a feeling their next conflict was going to be far, far worse.

CHAPTER NINE

ZAGAN

*Z*agan proverbially licked his wounds in his private quarters. He sat at his desk in front of a burning fire. His book of atonements sat open as he fingered the page with the list of witches and warlocks at his disposal. Only one name was missing from his ledger. He had yet to land that one, but it was on his to-do list. Especially as he pondered his recent defeat. Sadie may have won the battle, but the war was going to come quicker than she thought.

And I will win. I will have her and her power.

He brushed his finger against some of his more prized possessions reserved especially for Sadie when she would inevitably succumb to his power. Special rings infused with curses to remove willpower, and a choker designed to weaken her physical and magical strength.

Ultimately, Zagan didn't consider the defeat a loss as it was really a stale-mate. They were evenly matched, and he had underestimated Sadie's strength as well as his sons' devotion to her. He wouldn't make that same mistake again.

He rested on the assumption that showing up to her fortress and presenting himself as a threat would make her quake and quiver, grovel at his feet, and swear fealty. That she would see his power and the size of this army and agree to be his.

Yet she refused him.

For now.

No matter. He still had some tricks up his sleeve to get her under his control.

A knock echoed through the room, followed by the scratching latches of the door. Zagan rolled his eyes. "What now?" His voice boomed through the room.

"M-m-master, there is a matter that needs your attention."

Zagan recognized the tiny voice as the imp he enslaved as a child. He turned his gaze onto the creature and smirked as he quaked where he stood.

Pathetic.

"What is the matter that desperately needs my attention at this moment?" Zagan asked, allowing the irritation to filter through his voice as he did love it when his subjects trembled before him.

"The g-g-guards on the west wing missed their check-in."

"You stammering idiot! This is what you interrupted me for? I have captains in charge for a reason." He stood with the intent of beating the foolish creature into intelligence.

The imp cowered and pissed himself. The puddle reflected the fire near Zagan's desk. That was the last straw.

Zagan beat the creature as he squeaked and cried and begged for him to stop. With every hit and every kick, he felt better. Finally, the creature crumpled into a lump on the floor and remained quiet and still.

But he wasn't done. He motioned for the stone sentinels standing guard at the corners of his room to finish the job as he returned to his desk.

"Service!" he screamed.

Moments later, another imp entered the room and gawked at the creature in a mess on the floor. This one gazed at Zagan with fear but didn't dare address him directly.

"Clean this mess up," Zagan said. "And ensure no one enters this room under any circumstances."

The creature nodded and silently went to work.

Zagan returned to his thoughts.

He stroked the thin layer of facial hair that covered his chin and stared at the fire.

Where was I? Ah, yes. The battle with Sadie.

She chose all of his sons despite his warning not to pick any of them. The insolence of that woman would be taken care of soon enough. However, he knew his sons were strong individually. What struck him with surprise was how well they had worked together. Each of them had complemented the other in a way he imagined all of his soldiers did.

In a way, he was proud.

But the image of them fighting by the demon queen's side ate a him, making his blood boil.

He pounded his fist on the desk in front of him. The little imp whimpered. He shifted his dark gaze to the creature and smiled to himself as it cowered. Imps, to him, were ultimately useless creatures. But they were efficient enough slaves to keep them around. The entertainment they provided proved valuable in his reflections, though.

He should have killed the rest of his sons when he had the chance. But the bastards ran as soon as word of Cedric's death hit them.

Cowards. None of them deserved his throne. No one but him.

But he could see himself sharing the throne. Especially with Sadie. She would be his. Only his.

Her power, her sway, her surprising capability for a human… and if she continued to refuse him, he would make sure no one would have her.

Not even his sons.

Perhaps, he could right her mind by making her spend a few months in his dungeon. One he was sure rivaled even the great demon queen's.

He chuckled to himself as he imagined her cowering at his feet, begging for his mercy. It gave him a rock-hard erection, which he hadn't felt in years. He wouldn't hurt her, of course. Just deprive her of the very things she had learned to love. Things he would give back to her little by little.

In time, she would be his queen. And her power would be his.

He formed a plan to increase his numbers. He was going to take his time and make sure he had everything he needed to ensure his victory. For starters, the witch that continued to evade his advances. He would force her into his service by any means necessary. And his selection of demons in the void were excellent spies and assassins. He would call on all his allies and use them against the demon queen.

Sure, it would also give the queen time to rally her forces, but she didn't appear to have many beyond those ifrits, and he had allies of his own. Powerful ones. And he had a way of ensuring no one could say no to him.

When the moment was right, he would strike. She would either fall or be his.

He wouldn't accept any other outcome.

CHAPTER TEN

SADIE

On the way to her bath, Sadie checked on Steele. He was sitting up in his bed, and healing, but the process was so much more agonizingly slower than Sadie liked it to be. She wanted him at his best *now*.

He performed rather well during the battle, despite his grave wounds. She recalled how he took out several skeletons and goblins with his ability to cause his enemies to see horrific things, *feel* horrific things. Sadie shuddered as she remembered him using his ability against her.

Despite the odds that seemed stacked against him currently, he still fought for her. She just wished it wasn't with his life. She wanted to change the outcome of the events that landed him in bed, but she couldn't.

Still, she appreciated that he fought so ferociously for her and for their home. And she was ever grateful that he watched her approach the bed with all the love that he had for her in his intense gaze. She carefully sat next to him. He smiled at her, settling her nerves.

"Don't fret, my dear. I'm improving minute by minute. It won't be much longer before you have me back as you wish."

Sadie narrowed her eyes on him, perturbed by his constantly reading her mind. But at least he was healing, and his humor and normal carefree attitude was back. That helped to release the tension in the muscles in her neck and shoulders. "Well, at least you are sitting up and your humor has returned."

He shrugged. "It would take a lot more than my father's grunt soldiers to take me down."

"You're delirious. You really have no idea how close to death you were, do you?"

"Of course," he said. "But I'm not dead, am I?" He winked.

Sadie shook her head. "Not yet."

"Thank you, for your help." He took her hand into his and rubbed his thumb along her skin.

"Any time," she said, voice soft. She smiled.

"Although, if you really want me to heal faster... as a demon who prides himself on his sexual prowess," he placed his hand on his chest, "a little romp between the sheets would help do that just fine."

Sadie shook her head. *Always the sex fiend.*

But she smiled and stood from the side of the bed to climb over him. His eyes darkened as his hands gripped her hips. She leaned lower to kiss him. He deepened the kiss, and she allowed him to pull her closer. The need for him grew within her, and she knew she needed to stop before she allowed things to go too far and injure him all over again.

Finally, she pulled away before she could lose herself completely.

Steele leveled his gaze on her, and a light of confusion flashed in front of them.

"That's all you get for now." She stood and left to go take her bath.

SADIE

*T*he bath felt amazing. She always marveled at how the water constantly stayed at the perfect temperature. It was almost as though it obeyed her need to relax and ease the ache in her muscles. She was still really sore from battle and had gotten plenty of cuts and scrapes herself, which had healed quickly. But the ache was still there, and the bath soothed them away.

As she relaxed, she thought about her men and the

many comforts they offered her. She was grateful to have them, and the things they did for her. Many times without question. She loved how protective each of them was of her, and that helped to soothe her. She loved them with all she had in her, loved getting closer to them. Most of all, they were the most powerful allies she could ever ask for.

Sadie felt a presence enter her bathroom. She opened her eyes to find Mordecai solidifying from his shadow form. Inside *her* bath tub. A few curses sat on the edge of her tongue, but as soon as she set her gaze on his naked form, covered in thick muscles and toned skin, they disappeared. Sigils and tattoos covered his entire form.

He smirked. "Gonna kick me out now?"

She wasn't so sure she could, much less wanted to.

He seemed encouraged by her silence and lifted his hands filled with bubbles. He rubbed them along her arms, from her shoulders to the tips of her fingers. Then he shifted closer to her, rubbing her back and her front, massaging her breasts as he kissed along her collar bone.

Every touch of his hands, as he grazed them along her skin, sent shocking sensations through her body and filled her with not only warmth but *need*.

He chuckled. "Speechless? Interesting, Captain."

She smiled and said, "Don't get too comfortable or used to coming to me during my private time. That is still a rule of mine, and one you especially seem fond of breaking, much to my chagrin."

"I have yet to hear a complaint," he said as he continued to touch, rub, and kiss her.

She giggled and said, "I just haven't figured out the right moment to kick you out yet."

"Bet you can't." He settled his gaze on her and she became consumed with how deep and intense it was.

She allowed him to continue for just one minute longer and said, "I bet you I can."

"Challenge accepted." He kissed her deeply and his hand drifted to between her legs.

Sadie let out a soft sigh as she arched her back and felt a little bit more of her give in.

Mordecai kissed the space between her breasts and slipped his fingers inside her. She moaned. He took a breast into his mouth and sucked on her nipple while his other hand wrapped around her back, pulling her closer to him.

He abandoned her breast to ask, "Still want to kick me out?"

"Haven't decided yet," she panted out. But she wasn't going to. She couldn't. It felt too good to stop now, and she loved the way he was making her feel.

He chuckled and removed his hand to pull her closer, sliding her onto his lap. The water sloshed around them, and she felt his erection press against her belly. He kissed her, deep and passionate, leaving her lips to trace along her jawline and neck. He nibbled the spot of skin between her neck and collarbone, and she moaned again. Her legs twitched as her clit rubbed against his shaft.

His hands gripped her hips, and his shaft rubbed against her again.

Yes. Yes. More!

She clutched handfuls of his hair and gyrated along his shaft as pressure built between her legs. But just before she could gain that sweet release, he stopped her and adjusted himself to allow her to slide onto his erection.

She slowly let him fill her, and when she had settled with him completely inside her, he groaned.

"Dammit, Sadie. Don't stop now."

She smiled, feeling powerful and in control as she slowly moved up and down. His dick pulsated within her, and his fingers dug into her hips.

"Mmm…" he growled out and that made her need grow even more.

She quickened her movements, little by little until the pressure grew too great and released as she buried her face into the crook of his neck moaning.

He let out a dark, satisfying chuckle. "I told you, you couldn't kick me out."

She laughed and slapped his shoulder. "It's not too late, you know."

He shook his head. "Oh, we're already past all that."

Gripping her tighter, he stood and carefully stepped out of the tub. He carried her to her bed and laid her down, allowing himself to slide out of her so she could get adjusted.

Once she did, he wasted no time climbing on top of her, sliding an arm under her leg and pulling it over his shoulder. He hovered over her and stared into her eyes, seemingly looking for something that told her to stop. She glared at him.

He smiled, shook his head, and entered her.

At first, his thrusts were slow and gentle. That was all fine and dandy, but she wasn't fragile. She wanted what he could give with no holds barred.

"Harder," she demanded. "Give me all you got."

He gave her a questioning look. She bit her bottom lip and nodded.

"Okay." He didn't seem so sure she could handle it.

Well, she would show him.

His thrusts increased, harder, wild, savage. And she loved every moment of it. She needed more. She didn't want to stop. The bliss was too amazing, and this was exactly what she needed. The pressure built again and released. He grunted and warm liquid gushed inside her, and she was amazed at how she could orgasm at the same time.

Panting, they exchanged tender, more relaxed kisses. Mordecai pulled out of her and lay next to her. She curled into his body and breathed in his scent. He pulled her in closer and pressed his lips to her forehead.

As their breathing evened, Sadie's eyes grew heavier. She thought of how wonderful it was to be with him like that and how she felt even more connected to him now that she had.

Her last thought was of how she wouldn't have changed a thing.

CHAPTER ELEVEN

SADIE

*I*n the morning, Sadie and Mordecai found the other three princes eating breakfast and bantering back and forth. She smiled, warmed by the love the brothers shared. She loved them too, more and more each day. She especially loved that Steele appeared to be completely healed.

Relief flooded through her.

Kaiser laughed. "Seriously, your face though."

Steele shook his head and a big smile stretched his lips. "You should see some of the faces you make. Terrifying, really."

Damien sat back and shifted his gaze between his two brothers laughing along as they took turns making fun of their battle faces.

Sadie said, "I'm glad you are all having fun. And especially glad to see you up and around, Steele."

"I told you it wouldn't be long." He winked and took a seat at the table and grabbed an apple from the bowl at the center. He kicked up a leg on the edge of the table and tossed the apple between his hands. Ever relaxed and at ease.

"I, too, am relieved," Mordecai said as he approached his brother and squeezed Steele's shoulder before taking his own seat at the table.

Sadie joined everyone at the table, and Hobson served breakfast consisting of poached eggs, toast, and thick pieces of ham. He also placed a small bowl of fruit at the top of each plate.

"Tea, Your Majesty?" Hobson asked.

"Yes, please." She smiled and waited for him to finish pouring the tea into her cup before picking it up and blowing into the steaming liquid. She took a sip. "Mmm."

"I'm pleased you find it satisfactory," he said then moved to a spot along the wall while everyone ate.

That made Sadie wonder if Hobson ever found the time to eat and why he never joined them during their meals. "Hobson, care to join us?"

He pursed his eyebrows and his mouth parted slightly. "I-I couldn't possibly—"

"Nonsense," she said. "If you are hungry, please, join us and eat." She gestured to an available seat.

Hobson hesitated and then slowly moved to the table and sat down. He seemed unsure of what to do with himself, and Sadie wondered why he never got the opportunity to participate in the meals. Perhaps Hecate thought herself above him. To Sadie, he was an equal. Not her slave.

"Thank you, Sadie," he said and helped himself to the platters holding the food.

"Absolutely." Her attention shifted between her men.

They had barely scraped by the battle with Zagan by the skin of their teeth. She had been so focused on his visit that she wondered if her men felt a little neglected. She decided to spend a little one-on-one time with each over the next few days. Besides, having nearly lost Steele in the fight, she wanted to make sure she got a little more time with them individually. She missed having some of that down time as well.

Once everyone finished their breakfast, Damien said, "I'm going to go check out the barrier and do some repairs to it."

"Can I come with you?" she asked.

He smiled and nodded. "Absolutely."

SADIE

*T*hey walked outside the perimeter of the forests, checking for any signs of Zagan and his scouts while reinforcing weaker areas in the barrier. Though both of them were battle ready, they didn't seem to let that get in the way of enjoying the time they had with each other.

She absolutely loved the way she felt when she spent time with him. How powerful she felt with him around. Unstoppable. Untouchable. She relished in that feeling and couldn't help the smile that came to her face.

"I love it when you smile," he said. "I can understand why. You give me things no one ever could."

She stared at him and cocked her head to the side, overwhelmed by curiosity. "Oh yeah? Like what?"

He stopped and turned to face her. His hand gently cupped her cheeks. "You give me something to protect and cherish and a reason to live. You make me feel things no one else has. You move me…"

She kissed him. And he deepened the kiss, pushing her against a tree and pressing against her body. Fire ignited within her and she gripped fistfuls of his shirt in her hands. He moved his hands behind her head and wove his fingers through her hair.

She moved her hands to his shoulders, wrapping her arms around his neck. He gripped the back of her legs and pulled her up. She wrapped her legs around his waist and he squeezed her tightly to him.

Sadie grew dizzy. And just before she gave in to her need, she pulled back, panting.

"We should stop," she said.

"Why?" he growled out, eyes swirling red. He pecked the tip of her nose.

She giggled. "There will be more time for this. For now, we need to focus on training, maintaining the barrier, and finding a way to defeat your father."

He sighed, and they rested their foreheads together. After a few moments to catch their breath, he gently set her on her feet and made sure she was steady before letting go of her.

"My father is not to be taken lightly. It will take a great deal of training and planning to get close to defeating him. He's callous, ruthless, and does whatever he can to make sure he reigns supreme."

"I saw as much during the battle," Sadie said as they began walking along the barrier again.

Little creatures scurried through the underbrush as they walked. Some of them she caught short glimpses of before they disappeared. Damien held her hand and they scanned the magic of the barrier for more weak spots. Finding one, he released her hand and knelt, focusing some of his magic into the barrier, strengthening the area before returning to her, and took her hand again.

"Don't underestimate him, Sadie. He is powerful, using magic from whatever sources he can gain it from. He can wield weapons most couldn't touch without dying. He's a force to reckon with."

"So, we will become a greater force."

"How do you suppose we do that?" he asked as Sadie found a spot in the barrier and added her magic to seal the hole and fortify the area.

"Beating him at his own game," she said matter-of-fact.

He said, "He's a master at war. Sheer strength and will won't be enough to take him down. It won't be easy, but I think it can be done. He constantly feeds on the souls of his enemies, demon or otherwise, to gain more power and maintain his strength. That makes him nearly unstoppable."

Sadie's ears perked at that. *So that is his weakness.*

If she could find a way to exploit that, she could possibly defeat him.

"Is there a way to disconnect a demon from the souls he's eaten?" she asked.

"If there is, no one has figured out a way yet. That is for certain. I myself have never thought of that. But that is a great idea to pursue. Very resourceful of you."

She held her head a little higher. "Thank you."

"Even if we do succeed in figuring out a way to do that, the five of us still wouldn't be strong enough to take on my father. It will take more than just an army to overcome him. Defeating Mara was difficult enough with the daggers we had to find."

Sadie nodded, taking that into consideration and said, "In that case, I better get to work on training. The stronger I am, the better prepared I'll be to fight. And I tend to think better while training."

He pulled her into him and kissed her deeply. He murmured into her neck, "I would go crazy if anything happened to you."

Her knees grew weak and she got dizzy in the wake of his strong arms around her.

She had to train, think, and formulate a plan with the new information she just found out about Zagan.

But she just couldn't resist the way he made her feel. So, for a moment longer, she delighted in the feeling, laughed, and kissed him.

"Stay with me longer," he said, voice low. There was a hint of pleading in his words.

"The longer I stay here with you, the less time I have to train and even less time left before Zagan returns." She pried herself from him, smiled, and winked before turning and heading back to the fortress.

As she walked, she thought about her men and how they each demanded more and more time with her. Sex with her. She sighed.

Having an empire to run was almost exhausting enough, especially with all the wars that kept knocking on her doorstep. If she devoted herself to giving in to the men, satisfying their sexual appetites would turn into another full-time job. But it was fun to keep teasing them and leaving them wanting more. She demonstrated her control when she made them wait.

That was fun too.

She decided she would keep them wanting more. Besides, the sex had always been worth the wait.

That thought pulled her lips into a smile.

CHAPTER TWELVE

MORDECAI

*M*ordecai met Sadie in one of the many halls of the fortress. He smiled, as she did in greeting. As she passed by him, he hooked his arm around her and pulled her in close.

She laughed. "You beast, let go of me!"

"Never." His voice came out even. And he meant it. He could never let her go. Not in any sense of the word.

"I am going to go train now. If you would, please get Kaiser and Steele, and help Damien finish the barrier."

He frowned and released her. He could never tell her no when she requested anything of him either.

"Make sure you dispatch of any scouts that Zagan may have hanging around as well, please." She turned and headed down the hall, to her favorite training spot. She faced him and walked backward as she said, "In fact, take care of anything else that could threaten our safety and home while you're at it."

He bowed at the waist slightly and said, "Anything you wish, Captain."

She laughed, shook her head, and turned, continuing down the hall.

He stared at her rump as she moved, watching her until she turned the corner at the end. With a sigh, he set out to find his brothers and take care of the task.

~

MORDECAI

*A*fter the famous retelling of the first fight he and Kaiser had gotten into, the brothers shared a laugh.

"Man, Cedric was so angry we broke his staff," Kaiser said, shaking his head.

Mordecai pointed at him and said, "You mean the staff *you* broke."

"You grabbed it," Kaiser said and gave his brother a playful push. "I was just defending myself."

"Uh-huh. We'll go with that, even though you and I know damn well what really happened." Mordecai pushed Kaiser just as playfully.

Those were the days. Back when Cedric was the

big brother, keeping him and the others out of trouble and off Zagan's rampaging war path that happened every time the boys were too loud and rambunctious. Before their father shattered their family by removing the glue keeping the four remaining princes together.

Now, Sadie had become their glue.

That made Mordecai think about how they all separated after Cedric's death and reunited when Sadie became queen.

"Do you think we would be here right now, doing what we're doing if Sadie wasn't responsible for keeping us together?" he asked, without realizing he had spoken out loud.

"Duh," Steele said. "Are you new here?"

Mordecai smiled, but it bothered him that it took Sadie to reunite him and his brothers. But, at the same time, he was ever grateful for that. Not that he would dare speak those words out loud.

"Sadie is amazing like that. Not at all what I originally expected," Damien said.

"Yeah she is," Mordecai agreed. "Which is why I want to make sure each of you truly love her and will do whatever it takes to make sure she has a healthy, long rule."

"It's not like she's like Hecate, Mordecai," Kaiser said. "Sadie is probably even stronger than she was."

Each of his brothers agreed. Even Mordecai sensed the power growing within her.

Steele asked, "What do you think will grow first?"

Each of them turned their attention toward Steele.

"Horns, wings, or tail?" he added.

"Why does that matter?" Mordecai asked.

He shrugged. "Curiosity killed the cat."

"Yeah but knowing you," Damien said, "satisfaction brought him back."

Steele winked, snapped his fingers, and pointed at his brother. "You got that right. So, how about it. Maybe we can orchestrate a wager?"

"No!" Mordecai, Damien, and Kaiser spoke at once.

Steele held up his hands in defense. "Okay, just for fun. What do you think will grow first? I'm gonna say tail."

Kaiser said, "I vote horns."

Mordecai doesn't really see the point in this game, but to entertain his brother, he said, "wings."

Steele giggled with boyish enthusiasm as he said to Damien, "What about you, brother?"

"No. It shouldn't matter what grows first. And it's stupid to take bets on it, fun or not. Sadie is perfect regardless."

"No one is arguing that with you," Kaiser said.

Steele added, "Right. It's just a fun little bet. That's all. Honestly, if I may say so, the four of us couldn't care less what grew first, if anything at all. It was merely a curiosity, brother. Something fun to break the pitiful talk of old childhood games."

A sensation prickled through Mordecai and he paused. He looked to each of his brothers, all standing alert and at attention.

Good. They felt it too.

Each of them turned to stare into the shadows, searching for anything out of place.

There. He spotted movement and the tell-tale glow of magma.

Hellhound. And he prowled near the gate of the fortress.

Mordecai shifted into shadow and floated closer as the hellhound sniffed at the gate, growled, and started digging under it.

Before he could reach the creature, four more showed up from within the shadows. He heard footsteps stomping the ground from behind him, and he found assurance in knowing his brothers followed him.

"Those are father's dogs," Kaiser said. He would know. He had many encounters with them over the years and ones not soon forgotten with the screams Mordecai had to endure during the many, long, sleepless nights of his childhood.

Zagan probably sent the dogs out to find a way into the gate and report back. But not alone. There were imps too, somewhere. Spineless bastards.

They had a problem, and Mordecai was going to make sure they wouldn't get in.

"They're trying to get into the gates," Kaiser said, voice shaking.

Fat fucking chance.

"You know what to do Steele," he said and seeped through the gate, stopping behind the dogs.

Meanwhile, Steele did his thing and Mordecai could see the faint, ghostly outline of the images of him and his brothers stalking the creatures. He moved into position and waited for the right moment.

Kaiser's hands started to glow with red flames. Damien stood by with his sword in hand, waiting for the signal to hop through the gate and kill these dogs.

The illusion was set. Mordecai was at the ready. Time to go.

Damien charged. Kaiser shot flames at the dogs to aid in distraction. Mordecai solidified and drew his staff from the shadows. They attacked.

Mordecai swung his staff, sweeping the closest hellhound to him off its feet. The creature yelped, catching the attention of one of its pack mates. It lunged at him, scratching his leg. Deep gashes tore through his armor and flayed his skin. Biting back the pain, Mordecai thumped the dog on its head.

Damien jabbed at a hound between slats within the gate and Kaiser tossed another stream of fire to distract the other two.

Steele released his illusion as Mordecai looked

passed him, watching Sadie approach with a fierce march.

"Enough!" Sadie shouted, and all four princes looked to her.

The hellhounds instantly submitted to her, cowering, whining, and rolling on their backs, revealing their bellies like little lap dogs of death.

"I can use these hellhounds. See?" She gestured to them. "They're obedient to me."

"Sadie," Damien said. "Our father sent these creatures. If you take them from him, you'll only be angering him more. Tread carefully."

She shrugged. "His loss. Besides, look at them. They're so stinking cute! Maybe they will get along with Pyra?"

Mordecai shifted into shadow and seeped back through the gate a split-second before Sadie opened them and let the hounds in. They ran to her, barking and yelping. She giggled, turned around, and headed back to the fortress.

"You know this is just the beginning," Mordecai said to his brothers.

Damien nodded. "He'll send more and more, weakening our defenses little by little before his big attack."

"Then he'll come for her hide," Steele said. "Add it to his collection in his throne room."

"Over our dead bodies," Kaiser said.

They began to walk back, exchanging a few

commendations for a job well done. Mordecai was relieved he and his brothers could work so well together. It felt good. Like old times. And he owed that to the woman he loved.

She really was the glue for them now. And with that realization came the fact that he would rather die than let his father touch a hair on his woman's head. He stopped following his brothers long enough to look back along the horizon.

He knew his father's scouts were out there, and another troop was on their way. His father was a cunning little bastard and would likely wait until everyone's guard was down before they arrived. Meanwhile, he would do whatever he could to make sure Sadie and his brothers were safe.

CHAPTER THIRTEEN

SADIE

The next morning, Sadie made her way to the courtyard to train. As she entered her favorite training spot, Steele was there. She watched him move, his torso laid bare and the muscles stretched and moved with each motion he made. The light danced off his golden skin and he used his wings to aid in his momentum, which impressed her as she had wondered if they hindered movement.

She caught a glimpse of the scar from his latest injury. The one that nearly killed him. She frowned but shrugged it off. He was fine now. And that was what mattered.

His expression was focused. She wondered what he thought about as he trained. Her warrior. So serious. So fierce. She wanted to share in that.

She smiled as the urge to spar with him overtook

her wonder. That would give her an opportunity to further unify their ability to fight side by side. Like he did with his brothers.

Moving from the spot where she stood, she walked into the courtyard and waited for him to notice her.

He spun with a jab and a side kick. His eyes caught hers, and he smiled.

"Hey, gorgeous," he said.

She took her ready stance. "Hey, handsome."

He immediately took his stance and Sadie lunged. Laughing, he easily dodged the blow that would have hit him square in the jaw. "I love it when you're feisty."

She faked a left jab and did a front kick to his groin, which he avoided. "Not fair to cheat, Steele."

He shrugged, and a debonair smile pulled on his lips. "I am a demon." He winked then dashed to the side, swooped Sadie off her feet, and rolled to the ground, landing with him on top. "Demons don't fight fair." His words came out soft, deep, alluring.

She stared into his green eyes as they swirled with tinges of red, and she felt the gentle scratches on her mental barrier. He kissed her, and she let him in.

Visions of what the sparring session could lead to floated through her mind and she loved every idea. But she wouldn't give in. Not just yet.

She pushed him up, hooked her leg around his waist and pulled him down, rolling on top of him as she sat up and narrowed her eyes on him. "Steele. Focus."

He chuckled, and she couldn't help but join in. "But I am focused."

"On training," she said, playfully slapping him on the chest. *Always a one-track mind.*

He feigned injury and bucked her off him. She ducked and rolled, twisting at the landing to face him. He charged. Sadie side-stepped to avoid being barreled into and turned in time to duck a punch to her cheek.

"I'll make a bet with you," he said, holding up one finger.

She narrowed her eyes on him, already figuring what he was going to lead to. The same thing he always tried. Getting her in bed. "And what's that?"

"If I defeat you, I get whatever I want." He smiled, bobbing his eyebrows.

Sadie chuckled and shook her head. "And if I win?"

"You get to do to me whatever you wish." He spread his arms out to the sides.

She propped a hand on her hip and leveled her gaze on him, trying to be serious but knowing he probably saw right through her façade. "Steele, if you don't behave yourself, I'll cut this session short." Then, again, she felt more serious about that than she originally thought. They needed to train together. She needed to learn how he moved and reacted, and he needed to do the same.

He shrugged. "I'll take that as a yes."

Her eyebrows knitted together. "Wha—"

He charged her, cutting off her words so she could quickly run away from him.

They shared in a laugh as he chased her around the courtyard. Despite her need to train, she loved how Steele made her feel so carefree and happy. It made things easier to handle, somehow. The way he always took things with a grain of salt instead of being so uptight, balanced the gravity of planning ways to take Zagan off her radar and combat training. He helped her see that it was good to mix things up a bit and have a lighter heart.

Damn she loved him.

And she couldn't run from him forever. Though she knew he could catch her if he really tried. He just wanted to see her have a bit of fun. Still, she needed to think of a way to win this bet she didn't really agree to. The wall to her fortress was just ahead. It had vines and ivy climbing up the stone, and she could use that as a good foot hold.

But that wouldn't be enough to win the bet.

She conjured her shadow sword and ran up a wall, back flipping so that she could land behind Steele. He turned, and she held the point of the blade at him. He raised his hands in surrender, and a cocky grin stretched his lips.

She winked. "I win. Now, let's train."

He nodded and went to collect his own sword and stood in the center of the courtyard, waiting for her. She arrived, took her ready stance, and waited. Steele smirked and attacked.

Each move he made, she parried and countered. She knew he took it easy on her, and she appreciated that. She needed the practice anyway, and this was helping her to learn how he moved. She focused her strikes to the side, where he left himself the most open, but that wasn't a vulnerability as he managed to parry those attacks and gain advantage on her.

Good, he's learning too.

As they trained, her thoughts drifted to her new hellhounds. Maybe she should train with them too. They would definitely hold their own in a fight, especially in the upcoming war with Zagan. Getting practice in with them would ensure her hold over them and she could learn what they could do, decide how to best employ them, and build on her connection with them all at the same time.

"It's dangerous when you get lost in your thoughts," Steele said as he swirled out of the way of another one of Sadie's advances.

She lowered her sword. "What do you think about

training with the hellhounds?" she asked, ignoring the jibe.

"You prove my point," he said and lowered his sword. He rubbed the back of his head and sighed. "Lay it on me."

She leveled her gaze on him and hoped that he would take her question seriously, for once.

He stopped as well and nodded in thought. "Zagan has a few packs loyal to him. And, like everything and everyone else, they're completely expendable to him. You would likely need more than the few you have to make any real impact in a fight with him."

"Well, they're not expendable to me," she said. "Plus, we need all the help we can get."

"Very well. I don't recommend doing battle drills with them. They could get carried away and hurt you on accident. You could, however, practice on commands like you do with Pyra. Bonding with them will make them extremely loyal to you."

Sadie nodded and decided she would fit some time in with them after her training. The sooner she got started, the better.

Steele continued, "You know my father has a cruel nature about him. And he has a nasty habit of not accepting someone's 'No' when he gets one. He will do everything in his power to seek his vengeance for you turning him down."

He stepped closer as she opened her mouth to

speak, and he placed a finger over her lips. She narrowed her eyes on him. "Let me finish, would you?" He chuckled under his breath and shook his head and removed his finger.

He gazed at her as though he waited for her to respond. She nodded.

Satisfied, he said, "I promise, I will do everything I can to keep harm from coming to you. I have allies I can call on. Succubi. I just don't know how far that will get me."

She asked, "Why?"

"Because the usual price for their help and alliance is sex." He winked at her.

Sadie tried to force down that bubble of jealous anger that pooled in her gut. She clenched her fists and took in a steadying breath. Letting it out, she relaxed her hands and said, "Well maybe they will accept a different form of payment. Perhaps we can sway them with land, gold, or something that would benefit them."

He nodded. "I'll see what I can do." He gently cupped her cheek and leaned in to kiss her. Before his lips met hers, he said, "Don't worry, Sadie. I belong to you now. You're the only woman I want to be with."

His lips were soft and gentle as he kissed her, and that made Sadie feel like his words weren't just meant for reassurance, but also a promise.

When he pulled away, he asked, "Shall we continue, then?"

"Let's," she said and smiled with anticipation of training with him more.

Of course, that also meant avoiding his sexual advances. Though she let him get away with a few of those as well. She couldn't help herself. The things she felt for him were just too powerful to avoid completely, and it helped that she used them as distractions.

Lunch time approached when they decided to end their session and get some food. Sadie's stomach growled in agreement and Steele laughed. He held out his arm for her and she took it, letting him walk with her to the dining hall.

CHAPTER FOURTEEN

SADIE

*S*adie laughed as Steele stood on top of the dining room table and, with grand gestures and a great deal of stretching the truth, retold his personal account of the fight with the hellhounds. They were all healed from the scratches they endured.

He kicked a goblet off the table. "He slammed the staff into the dog, knocking his hind legs from under him." He held up a finger. "But I could tell he put all his strength into it. Must suck to have that blow up in your face." He pouted.

His face lit up. "Oh, but here's the best part. The other hound had turned," he twisted in place, "and was staring at him like, 'why'd you do that?'" He took on the look of what Sadie considered a "puppy dog face."

Another roll of laughter filled the room.

Steele shifted on top of the table, crouched down,

and held his hands up like claws. "Then he was like, 'Eh? Pick on someone your own size,' and slashed," he quickly brought a clawed hand down, "Slicing your leg up pretty bad."

He hobbled the length of the table, pouting. He stopped at the edge, jumped down, and then spun around to bow.

"Is that how it happened?" Mordecai asked. "I seem to recall you standing around with this blank stare on your face."

Steele shrugged. "I was simply hoping the dog would bite a chunk out of you. Shorten you a bit. A very humbling height, I do believe."

The rest of the brothers joined in with their own retellings, and each one managed to poke fun at the others. The table was an utter mess at the end of it all. Food was scattered. Drinks were spilled, and poor Hobson stood off to the side shaking his head, frowning at the mess.

She watched the dramatic retellings. It was fun to be so at ease with her men, and to see them get along as brothers should, filled her heart with warmth. Each day that passed she found herself more and more appreciative of their presence and willingness to get along for her sake. But it seemed they truly enjoyed themselves as well as each other's company.

Once Kaiser finished his story, Sadie stood and said, "Regardless of how… comical your retellings are,

I still must know when enemies come to my gates. *Before* you start fighting them."

"Yes, of course," Mordecai said. "If we have time. Which, that time, we didn't."

Sadie nodded. "Fine. Just keep in mind my order for *next* time." She looked to each of the men pointedly as each one nodded. "Very well. Now, let's clean up this mess and move to the war room."

Once the table was cleaned and all the debris from the reenactments was over, the men followed her to the war room. After everyone was seated and looking at her expectantly, she took in a deep breath and said, "I need a plan of action against your father if we want any hope of defeating him."

Kaiser said, "There is a rumor about a weakness my father has, but I never figured out what it was. Cedric knew. I went to go ask him about it, but it was too late. Cedric was already dead."

"I have a band of warlocks," Mordecai said. "I could ask a few favors from them. They may be able to find out more about the weakness than I would know. I hated my father from the moment I could think for myself and I don't want to spend any more time talking about him than necessary."

Duly noted. She wouldn't force him to talk if he didn't want to. Though she wished he would, she also understood his hatred for his father and could appreciate wanting to avoid the topic. While he could do that, she couldn't.

"Could his weakness be consuming souls?" Sadie asked.

Damien shook his head. "I don't think that's it."

"Why not?" Sadie asked.

"It's more the strength he gains from the souls as he ages," Damien said.

Kaiser said, "I may have to disagree, brother. I recall a number of times when father's health declined suddenly and then the very same day, just later, he seemed to have bounced back with more strength and vitality than before."

"I've seen the same things," Steele said. "Always was curious about that."

"So, you both are inclined to believe that is a possible weakness we can exploit?" Sadie asked them.

"Yes," they said.

Steele added, "I will speak to the succubi queen on your behalf, and I'll barter for a different form of payment."

A pinched formed in Sadie's forehead at the reminder of the payment they usually required from Steele. She nodded.

"I also have allies I could get on our side," Kaiser said. "My strongest ally is the gorgon queen."

Damien said, "And I have witches, which would complement Mordecai's warlocks."

Things were starting to come together. They had a list of allies to choose from, but Sadie wasn't sure what they brought to the table as far as skills. Not to mention, there didn't seem to be a guarantee that any of them would come to their aid. She said, "Tell me what each of your allies can do if they were willing to help us."

"Succubi are very apt at distractions of the kinky kind," Steele said.

Sadie forced herself not to roll her eyes. At least she now knew why he and his allies got along so well.

"They are also vicious in fights, especially when protecting what they claim as theirs," Steele added.

Hmm... maybe they won't be so bad after all. She should meet them on the right foot, without preconceived notions in her head about what they had done with Steele before she came into his life. But she would be sure to lay some rules down beforehand. The question was of payment options beyond sex with Steele.

"What else can you tell me? What about their powers specifically?" Sadie asked, curious to know more. She wanted to know exactly what she was getting into when it came to his allies.

"Typically, they steal parts of human souls when they have sex with them. When they have sex with demons, they get a power boost. Essentially becoming stronger for about a week."

"Are you sure they can be trusted here?" she asked.

"If we come to an agreement, they wouldn't dare break it. They would know better."

Steele sounded serious and Sadie knew not to press further. She trusted him and believed him. That was enough.

Kaiser said, "My allies are creatures exceptionally skilled at ice magic. They're also considered harbingers of death. Having them on our side would do more in presentation than in battle, but that's not to discount their strength. They are ruthless and skilled on the field. Having them on our side would show my father we mean business and may give him a reason to reconsider."

Sadie liked the sound of them. Ice magic and death. Two things she needed on her side. Especially if they were considered threats against Zagan.

"Besides what I have already shared with you as far as witches and warlocks are concerned," Damien said, "having both in your arsenal would greatly increase our ranks with sheer force."

She nodded, remembering what he had shared with her, and she still looked forward to meeting a few.

This could work.

Renewed hope filled her. They had a chance at defeating Zagan if her princes could convince their allies to join them.

"Send the invites at once."

She called Hobson through her connection with the fortress.

He entered not long after. "Yes, Your Majesty?"

"Prepare the barracks for the soldiers, and the guest quarters for those who would appreciate and demand a more suited suite."

He nodded. "At once." He left to do her bidding as Sadie returned her gaze to her men.

This was exciting. They had a chance. And while her princes worked on gathering their allies, she would train the hounds and with her dragon.

"For the next few hours, I will be training with the hellhounds. You should all rest and focus on training once you are finished with your invitations."

They nodded, and Mordecai uttered a "Captain" before standing and leaving.

CHAPTER FIFTEEN

SADIE

The training with her hellhounds had gone better than expected. They seemed eager to please her and she rewarded them with left over meats from the kitchen. She had trained with them for several hours, both individually and as a group. They were such fascinating creatures to her. She was glad they responded well to her and obeyed her.

After she finished with her training, she needed some alone time to think. She decided to go to the fortress's back garden. To her sister's statue. She sat on the bench across from the statue and stared at the likeness, wishing that Blair was with her right then to give sisterly advice, tips on fighting with demons, and maybe even a hug.

"I miss you so much, Blair," she said, wishing the statue would somehow come to life and console her.

Blair's statue held a mageblade in one hand, like the one Sadie had used against the demoness Mara, and the statue's other hand presented an orb—Blair's last gift to Sadie, which had sent her to safety and condemned Blair to death. Sadie's chest tightened at the thought, and she held back tears.

Above her, the crystals in the ceiling sparkled and twinkled as the night settled in. She wrapped her arms around herself.

"So much has happened, and I don't know what I'm doing. Just winging it." She laughed, thinking that would be something Blair would've done. However, since discovering Blair was a notorious demon hunter, she knew better. Her sister was badass and had died protecting Sadie.

"Don't get me wrong, I love my life. I don't have any regrets to speak of, really. It's just so much to handle sometimes. Who knew being queen would be so much work? Those royals on topside make this shit look easy."

She remembered that the amulet she wore around her neck, the demon queen's amulet, didn't bond with just anyone. It had rejected Blair, but why? Her sister had been immersed in this world, of monsters and demons, and she knew how to take care of herself. She would've made a formidable demon queen. But from the moment her sister slipped the amulet around her neck and had her whisked off to safety, the responsibility—fate—had fallen to her.

Whatever reason the amulet had for choosing Sadie, the one thing she was certain of was that she would honor Blair's sacrifice and keep it out of the hands of her enemies. Not only did she have a kingdom to look after, with loyal subjects like the fiery ifrits, but also her men. She loved that they were protective of her, and she fiercely felt the same about them. Hopefully, no more memorial statues would have to be erected in this quiet garden.

The shadows within the garden had grown thicker and darker. A light breeze floated around her, carrying the scent of petals and musk. That was Blair's perfume. Her favorite. A tear fell along her cheek and she wiped it away, the remnants feeling cold as the breeze blew against it.

"Thank you, by the way, for giving me this life. At first, I blamed you. I thought you hated me and cursed me to a tormented life. But not anymore. I then wondered how the hell you kept this from me and the rest of the world, but I have come to understand why you did. People would go nuts if they knew this stuff was real."

Sadie forced back a giggle as she envisioned the chaos that would consume the world above if demons had become common place. If they revealed themselves. Widespread panic, destruction, and martial law would be the first. But the world would slowly unravel.

Yeah, it's a good thing people aren't in the know.

"You did me a favor. Though, I wish you were really here with me, sharing in my spoils of war and enjoying this enormous fortress with me. Helping me keep these men in check." She sighed. "Now, if I could just keep demons from knocking down my door in an attempt to kill me, that would be a great bonus. But I've accepted my job. Both the good and the bad of it."

Sadie looked up again and thought about all the things she would be missing out on if Blair hadn't slipped the amulet around her neck and made her demon queen. She was definitely very happy her sister did.

She stood from the bench and slapped her hands on her legs. "I miss you. And I love you very much, sister."

With that, she made her way back to her room.

She sat on the bed and summoned Hobson. Ever dependable, he was there within the time it took her to remove her boots.

He knocked on the door and entered the room. "Yes, Your Majesty?"

She smiled. "I was hoping for some tea. Are you too busy?"

"Not at all, Your Highness. I'll fetch it at once." He turned to leave, but Sadie stopped him.

"Hold on a moment, please," she said.

His eyebrows rose. "As you wish."

She leaned forward and studied him for a moment. He seemed tired. She was concerned. "Are you well?"

"Perfectly. May I ask why?" he asked.

She shook her head. "We haven't had a moment to catch up with all the running around and training. I didn't want you to think I forgot about you."

If stone could blush, he just did. The grey of his cheeks darkened as if they were just wet from rain. "I appreciate your concern, Sadie, but I am fine."

She nodded, accepting his response. "Can I ask you about hellhounds?"

He strode into the room farther and she patted the spot on the bed next to her. He seemed to have hesitated, unsure of what to make of the offer, but she nodded, and he took the seat. "What would you like to know?"

She sat straighter, twisting slightly to face him more directly. "For starters, are there any wild packs around here?"

"There was a moderately sized pack that was known to come within the barrier of the fortress from time to time. But they never venture too close to the gates." He paused to think a moment then added, "I must inform you, hellhounds are highly difficult to gain loyalty from. The fact that you have done so well with the four you already have is remarkable. That's a good sign. I don't see you having any problems acquiring more if you desired."

"Thank you, Hobson," she said and rested a hand on his arm. "The hounds that would cross the barrier, do you think they are still there?"

He shook his head and shrugged. "Hard to say, they were last on the eastern side, if that helps."

She nodded. "Thank you, Hobson. I'll let you return to your duties."

He stood from the bed. "Shall I get your tea now?"

"If you don't mind," she said.

"Not at all." He excused himself from the room.

While she waited, Sadie drew herself a bath and had a long soak. Once she was out, the tea sat on her night stand next to her bed. She smiled to herself as she approached the cup, picked it up, and then took a sip.

Still warm. And so, so good.

Just the thing she needed right before bed.

CHAPTER SIXTEEN

SADIE

*K*aiser held out a blindfold for Sadie, waiting for her to agree to let him put it on.

She raised an eyebrow and crossed her arms over her chest. "I don't think so."

He dropped the hand with the blindfold to his side. "Why? We haven't had time to spend together in forever, it seems. You're always so pre-occupied. Let me have this one thing. It won't take forever."

His eyes. Those pleading, pretty brown eyes. She couldn't resist him. But she was just on her way to train, and if she skipped out on training today, she would have to force herself to double the time tomorrow, and she didn't have the time to do that. Missing training just wasn't an option.

He cleared his throat. "Please?"

Her eyes widened, and she feigned the look of shock. "Either I'm rubbing off on you or you're not Kaiser. Who are you? What have you done to my prince?"

He laughed, and she joined in with him. He asked, "So, what will it be?"

She paused to make him sweat a little more as she figured it wouldn't hurt to miss out on a little training. She would keep the time limit short and that was it. Long enough for him to show her whatever it was that required her to be blindfolded. A hint of disappointment crossed through his eyes, and she almost felt guilty for dragging the charade on for so long. "Very well."

He smiled and did a fist pump. Sadie chuckled and turned around so he could tie the blindfold over her eyes. Once done, he grabbed her hand and led her through a series of hallways and to one of her gardens.

Eventually, he instructed her to sit, and helped her lower to the ground. A few seconds of feet shuffling and a grunt from Kaiser as he sat down later, the blindfold was removed.

Sadie settled her eyes on the lavish spread of meats, cheeses, and fruits collected on plates and arranged in front of her on a picnic blanket. "Oh, Kaiser. I don't have time for a picnic. I have to train so I can be prepared to fight Zagan."

"There will be plenty of time for training later." He grabbed a napkin and laid it on her lap.

"There will also be plenty of time to have a picnic after we kill Zagan too. Kaiser, this is wonderful. Truly, it is. But I just can't afford to miss any training."

Kaiser growled. "Why is it always war, war, war with you? You're like a robot programed with that one directive. It's okay to take a break, you know. Hell, if you don't allow yourself to take a break, you'll go insane or be too damned exhausted to fight my father when he returns."

Sadie's fist clenched, and a pinch formed in the center of her forehead. "I'll have you kno—"

Kaiser leveled his gaze on her, eyes turning red. "Just sit down and relax for five damn minutes. Beheading of demons can start later."

She gave in. Not because he was getting angry, but because he had made a good point. She had been so focused on training that she hadn't thought about something as simple as food or relaxing. Plus, she had yet to have some time alone with him. Come to think of it, she felt a little guilty for neglecting him. That, and the effort he had put into the lavish display was impressive and thoughtful.

"Okay, but only five minutes." She winked.

He shook his head and propped an arm over his bended knee. "Deal. Now, let's dig in." He pulled out a bottle of wine and a glass from the other side of him and poured Sadie a cup of the sweet, red liquid.

She thanked him and took a sip, savoring the floral flavor that danced along her tongue.

Kaiser took a long swig of blood from a flask. He wiped his mouth with the back of his hand.

Sadie smiled at him, unaffected by the fact he drank blood. All of her princes did. It was a part of who they were, and she loved each and every single quirk and weird habit of theirs.

He caught her staring and asked, "Still weird you out?" He shook the flask to emphasize what he referred to.

"Not at all," she said. "It's sort of… fascinating."

He shook his head, smiling. "You are something else."

Sadie picked up a grape and plopped it into her mouth. The sweet juices squirted in her mouth. "Yeah, well, being thrown into the role of demon queen has forced me to quickly accept that there were changes and lifestyle choices I had to get used to."

"You did, indeed, adjust rather quickly. I'm impressed. You were suited for this role."

Sadie shrugged. "I suppose so. But I've always been able to think on my feet and roll with the punches. Never made much sense to get snagged on every change."

"You do get uptight though," he said and chuckled.

She smiled, knowing that was very true. "Nobody is perfect, Kaiser. Despite how much you think I am."

He poked her in the side and she jumped. "Yep. You're real."

She laughed. "What is that supposed to mean?" She took a piece of roasted meat and stuffed it into her mouth. The spices were robust with a hint of sweetness. She didn't know what kind of meat she ate, but it reminded her of the roasts her mom used to make over the holidays.

"It means I find that you are too good to be true sometimes. You were never what I would've expected for being human. It's freeing to be so captivated by you and still know you are real and haven't let this newfound power of yours go to your head." He ate some of the meat himself. Juices dribbled down his chin and he used the back of his hand to wipe his mouth.

Sadie's heart swelled with joy and love. He always had a way of making her feel desired by him. Coveted even. She sat the wineglass next to her and scooted closer to Kaiser. He responded by wrapping an arm around her and she leaned in to kiss him.

The way he kissed her always ignited passion within her. Her body warmed, and desire swam through her veins. She straddled him, pushing him to the ground and kissing him deeper. Pressure built between her legs, and she knew she needed to stop, but her body rebelled against her, pushing for more. Needing more.

But now was not the time.

She forced herself up and laughed. "If we keep at this, the world just may fall apart."

He reached for her, cupping the back of her neck with his hand and pulled her down. "Let the world fall for just a few more minutes."

She let him kiss her one last time. Dammit if she didn't want him to stop.

Once again, she pulled her lips away from his, but instead of climbing off him, she laid her head on his chest and listened to the rhythm of his heartbeats. She smiled, relishing the feeling he gave her.

She knew she had just fallen for Kaiser a little more. He had been with her since the beginning. And because of the devotion he showed, and the way he made her feel, there was no way in hell she would ever let anything happen to him.

Come what may, she would rather harm come to her than him, or any of her princes.

After a few moments of cuddling, Kaiser said, "You need to eat."

She groaned. "Do I have to?"

He chuckled. "If you want to build up and keep your strength, yes. Plus, it would be a shame for all this food to go to waste."

She sighed. "You're right. Too good to waste."

"Exactly."

Reluctantly, she climbed off of him and settled into the spot right next to him. They enjoyed the rest of the food and each other's company, spending the rest of the afternoon in bliss and love.

CHAPTER SEVENTEEN

SADIE

*J*ust before night settled in, Sadie decided to check the barrier around her fortress herself. On the way, she stopped and grabbed her hellhounds, hoping to get in some extra training with them and for the added protection since all her men were busy doing other tasks.

So far, everything looked good. She hadn't come across any weaker areas that needed refortification. Her hounds also kept looking to her for something to do, seemingly bored and itching for a job.

Pausing in her trek around the barrier, she decided to do some of the training she planned for and used the vines to create walls, forming a small labyrinth, keeping herself in the middle. Next, she used her mental connection with the creatures, sending them an image of where to stand and wait until her signal, having each of them start at different entrances.

She shot a ball of fire into the air, signaling to the hounds to find her as quickly as possible.

Growls and snapping teeth filled the night air as she waited for her hounds to sniff her out. Burning iron and sulfur filled the air mixed with the sounds of screeching metal and scratches. And quicker than she expected, they showed up, each meeting her at the same time as the others.

"Wow. That was quick." She gave each of them a pet and went to figure out how they solved her labyrinth in such a quick amount of time.

All she did was turn the first corner and it became clear to her. They burned holes through the walls...

Little cheaters.

In retrospect, she never clarified to them how to get through the maze. Just to get to her with haste.

She shrugged and smiled at her hounds for their ingenuity and ability to get around obstacles by any means possible.

"Well I guess I'll just have to be much more specific in my orders from now on, huh?" she said and laughed as they each barked at her and wiggled their butts. She shook her head.

She had an idea. And the hounds seemed willing to do more, which encouraged the idea further.

She dismissed what remained of the walls then

focused on creating an individual wall in front of each hellhound. Conjuring the vines, she wanted the wall to be thicker than before. It took some effort, and beads of sweat covered her forehead, but she had four of them up. She mentally instructed the hounds to stand in front of each.

They moved, making little growls that came out excited but raised the hairs on the back of her neck.

Next, she whispered, "Burn."

The hounds began to glow, turning almost white with the intensity of the heat. Sadie smiled.

Cool.

She then mentally told them to go through the wall. They barked in response and dove through the wall as if it were nothing. Gaping at their speed and the holes burned through the metal vine walls, she walked around to the other side and saw them shaking with happy excitement.

They deserved a treat, and she mentally sent Hobson an order of whatever suited a hellhounds pallet for as much.

But she wasn't done. She wanted to see how well their magic worked together. The remainder of the walls toppled to the ground, disappearing into ash and dirt. She conjured a single tower, as wide as she could muster and taller than her by a couple feet.

She slapped her thighs. The hellhounds rushed to her and sat, panting, at her feet. She mentally ordered them to face the tower, and on her mark, she shot a beam of fire into the vines. They heated to a red-orange glow, the smell of metal burning filled her nose.

She noted that they could burn through the vines faster than she could, which was something to be proud of. But what she really wanted to know was how much more powerful their magic could be combined. So, she mentally told the hounds to burn again. And she turned her fire to them, merging everything together, turning them blue.

The hounds charged. The tower fell, and they jumped over the smoking mass back to her side, eager for more.

The hellhounds instantly sat at attention, looking behind Sadie. She pursed her eyebrows and turned to see Mordecai approaching. He held his hands up in defense. "I know your time alone is important to you. I only wanted to see if I may join you."

She smiled and nodded. "Sure. I would love that." Maybe she should rethink her rule regarding her private time. But then again, he was very polite in his approach. Respect. That's what it was about.

He nodded and joined her side. "So, how is the training going?"

"Good. Have a little tweaking to do, though. I haven't found any weaknesses in the barrier so far," she said.

He slipped his hands in his pants and remained quiet. A small crease appeared in the center of his forehead. Sadie wanted to ask what concerned him, but she knew he would tell her when he felt the time was right. So, she slapped her legs and her hounds rushed to her side. She started to walk around the barrier again.

Mordecai kept up with her, still silent as ever. It wasn't like him to be so serious and less jovial. By now, he would have her pinned to a tree, side of the fortress, the ground, anything, and have his mouth on hers. Though she was uncomfortable with this unusual side of Mordecai, she decided to keep her mouth shut and wait for him.

The light in the underworld faded little by little in their walk.

Once they finished walking the perimeter of the barrier, Mordecai pulled on Sadie's arm to stop her and face him. His eyes were intense as they stared into hers. Her heart skipped a beat and forced back the urge to gulp.

"I belong to you. I belong to you alone. Whatever it takes—whatever I can do—to protect you and keep you safe. I will do without thought. You will never have to worry about my standing with you."

She opened her mouth to respond to his words, but he stopped her by pressing his lips to hers. The kiss was different. Deeper. Full of promise. Everything she had yet to feel with him, and everything she had felt before. But most of all, she felt loved, craved, wanted.

Before she completely melted into him, he pulled away and brushed her hair from her face. "We should go in before the shadows get darker and longer."

She looked around them and noticed that nightfall neared and agreed. It was getting late and dinner would be soon. Besides, the fortifications were strong and the wards active. They would be safe for the rest of the night.

"Lead the way," she said and smiled.

He took her hand and they walked back into the fortress together.

After putting her hounds in their stalls, she turned to Mordecai and said, "I need to get ready for dinner. I'll meet you there, okay?"

He nodded, kissed her once more, and left her to her lightheaded walk to her room.

CHAPTER EIGHTEEN

KAISER

*W*hile Sadie got ready for dinner, Kaiser took the opportunity he had alone with his brothers to have a few words with them regarding Sadie's safety from their father.

He found them all sitting in the library, gathered around the chess board. Mordecai and Steele attempted a match while Damien stood off to the side, watching with his legs crossed, leaning against the bookshelf and his arms folded over his chest. His lips were turned down at the corners, and his eyes seemed glazed over.

Once Kaiser entered the room, Damien lifted his gaze to him. "Come to watch the slowest match of a lifetime?"

Kaiser shook his head.

Steele said, "You're just jealous you didn't win the bet. Care to join in on the wager, Kaiser?"

He shook his head. "I'm not here for games. I needed a moment with you to discuss Sadie."

That got their attention. Mordecai and Steele abandoned their game and all three turned toward him.

He nodded. Good. "What is the plan to keep Sadie safe from our father?"

Mordecai snorted. "This again."

"You may have an issue with the general topic of our father," Damien said, "but keeping Sadie safe from all of his sneaky little advances should be of top priority. I myself have wondered the same thing."

"It's obvious," Steele said. "Kill him, duh."

"Yes, but how?" Kaiser asked. "We have each tried a number of times over the years. We have to find a different approach."

He thought about the time when his brother Cedric was killed at the behest of their father. How it had separated them, divided them, and set each of them against one another. That was the last thing Kaiser wanted. He had just gotten his brothers back. They were a unit again. Sadie had brought them together and made them all family once more.

Kaiser had suspected for some time that his father killed Cedric to separate him and his brothers. He was never a man that enjoyed family, love, or closeness. He was a hardened asshole who saw love as an unnecessary emotion and weakness.

Now, he was after the woman he loved. Though he knew it would be for the sake of gaining her power, just another pawn in his father's game of war, it would also break the brothers apart.

He would be damned if Zagan so much as split a hair on Sadie's head.

"Though I agree on killing Zagan, what exactly are you thinking? Babysitting?" Damien asked. "She'll never agree to that."

Kaiser shook his head. "She doesn't have to know exactly what is going on. She's too stubborn to go along with it. But she's smart too, so we have to be careful."

Silence settled between them for a few long moments. Finally, Mordecai asked, "What did you have in mind, exactly?"

Kaiser shrugged. "We can't let her go anywhere alone. That's too prime of an opportunity for any of Father's scouts to pass up."

"What about her demand for private time?" Mordecai asked. "We can't just show up each and every single moment she demands to be alone, can we?"

"No. Of course not," Kaiser said.

"Then we need to plan a way for her to get her time alone without our presence being known at the same point in time." Damien removed himself from the bookshelf and took a seat in a plush chair not far from the chess board.

Kaiser walked farther into the room and took a seat by an end table. "I agree."

Mordecai and Steele agreed as well.

"So, I suggest taking shifts," Steele said. "I'll go first."

"You're jumping ahead, brother," Kaiser said. "We need to take this slow and make the plan solid, then give out shifts." He turned to Damien, "When do you plan to take her topside?"

"Tomorrow evening."

Kaiser nodded. "Mordecai, you go with him. She'll need the both of you if anything goes down."

They nodded.

"That means you," he looked to Steele, "and I will stay behind. We'll welcome the first set of allies that are set to arrive while they are gone."

"And if she disagrees?" Mordecai asked.

"We'll reason with her until she sees that keeping someone behind to welcome the allies will be for the best," Damien said. "She'll see things as we do."

"What about the most important thing of all?" Steele asked. Once everyone looked to him, he continued, "Killing dear old dad."

"It's not like we haven't all known this day was

going to come eventually," Damien said. "It's time we handle him once and for all."

All the brothers agreed.

"He won't give up until he has what he wants," Kaiser said.

"He'll die when he comes again. We'll make sure he won't be a danger to Sadie anymore," Mordecai said, a dark promise sounded clear in his voice.

"Yes, but *how* is the question," Damien said.

The brothers stood around quiet and staring at each other, each one seemed to be waiting on the other to speak first.

"Sneak into his bedroom and slit his throat," Steele said. "Mordecai could do it with his shadow magic."

Mordecai shook his head. "If I thought it was going to be that easy, I would've already done it. And we wouldn't be standing here today."

"Steele, you could use your magic to create an illusion to distract father while Mordecai does the shadow thing," Kaiser said.

Damien stepped to the center of the room. "Ideally, we would all need to take part in it. Using all our skills together. Even then, it may not be enough. He has his sentinels standing guard at his doors. Taking them out would be difficult as they detect magic and will behead any one approaching without Zagan's word."

Hobson entered the room. "Dinner is ready."

Each of the princes thanked the gargoyle. Kaiser gave his brothers a pointed look, a silent promise that they would figure out a solution to dealing with their father.

At least, for now, they had a plan. Kaiser walked out of the room feeling more at ease with the direction they were headed in. With the charm he placed on Sadie's lower back, and at least two of his brothers with her at all times, they would be able to make sure Sadie wouldn't get hurt and remained safe from their father.

CHAPTER NINETEEN

SADIE

*L*ater that evening, after dinner, Sadie sat in her room staring at her clothing. Damien told her they were going topside tomorrow to meet the witch, Astrid. And she was so nervous. She had no idea what she wanted to wear or what she should wear. She went back and forth between keeping things casual and really spicing things up with some of her sexier outfits. She definitely didn't want to go in a fancy dress. That would be too much, and Damien had already warned her that they needed to remain as inconspicuous as possible.

Finally, she decided on a simple outfit of jeans, a t-shirt, and sweater with knee-high boots.

She sat on her bed, getting ready to crawl in for the evening, when a knock came on her door.

"Yes?" she said.

Hobson entered. "Sorry to bother you at such a late hour. I would have waited for a more appropriate time, but you have been so busy with preparations and training."

She shook her head and waved him off. "Don't worry about it. The hour is fine. What can I do for you?"

He sighed. "I'm worried about you."

"Why?" A pinch formed between her eyebrows.

"I have been around for quite some time. And I've learned things over the years. For one, the numerous stories regarding witches and warlocks being tricky creatures. Determining their loyalties, and whether they are good or evil, is difficult."

Sadie slowly nodded. She was touched that her butler cared for her in such a way. She loved him for that and wanted to reassure him that the course she was taking was the best one. One that only she could take.

"Okay. I understand your worry, but the princes would never suggest anything that could put me into danger. I'll be fine."

"Sadie, please," he said, hands folding in front of him as if in prayer. "I just don't want to see you get hurt. I wish there was another way for you to learn about them."

She stood and approached her gargoyle butler,

taking his hands into hers. "What can I do to reassure you that I will be fine?"

He pressed his lips together and shook his head. "Not meet them."

Wow. He didn't mince words. Rarely had the gargoyle ever requested anything of her, and he seemed adamant that she avoid meeting witches and warlocks.

"You know I can't do that," she said with a twinge of guilt at denying his plea.

His shoulders slumped, his gaze shifted to the floor, and he nodded. In a quieter, resigned voice, he said, "Please, remember you have inherited many enemies from Hecate. Many of whom have arsenals of witches and warlocks at their command. I urge you to be cautious and extremely careful in dealing with them."

"I will." She let go of his hands. "Besides, what sort of queen would I be if I sent everyone else to do my dirty work and never left the fortress, much less avoid fights that could get me hurt? The fights are mine to take care of, and I need to protect my home... and you."

His cheeks darkened in the way that stone did when wet. He grinned and nodded.

"I really appreciate your worry, and your help. I wouldn't know how to run this fortress if it weren't for you and your amazing knowledge and assistance."

"My pleasure, Your Majesty." He bowed his head.

"Is there anything else I can do for you? Anything else you needed?"

He shook his head. "I do wish you would reconsider the visit topside. However, I also understand your reasoning and stand behind your decision."

She nodded. "Well, thank you for coming and talking to me about your concerns. I want to encourage you to do so anytime. Regardless of what I'm doing."

"As you wish," he said.

"If you don't mind, I would like to get some rest now." She smiled.

His eyes grew wide and he seemed to have forgotten what he was doing or where he was. He quickly looked from side to side then back to her, and dropping his gaze, nodded. "Of course. Goodnight, Your Majesty."

"Goodnight, Hobson." She opened the door and saw him out. Once he left, she closed the door, leaned against it, and stared at the ceiling with a sigh. She was dizzy with the rotating information in her head.

She understood where Hobson was coming from, and she appreciated his concern. But she couldn't just be kept hidden away and let everyone she was charged with do everything for her. She refused to be that person. That was what she imagined Hecate must have been like—letting everyone do her dirty work while sitting on her throne with a cruel hand. No wonder the former demon queen was a lonely ghost haunting the south wing.

That wouldn't be her. No. She needed to fight her own battles, and that meant the grunt work involved too. There was no other way. She had to see the witches and warlocks for herself. She trusted Damien not to place her in danger, and Astrid wasn't aligned with any demon. Which meant she couldn't be all that evil, right?

Either way, she needed to find a way to defeat Zagan, rally forces in her favor, and fast.

Luckily, they were heading for what would be a promising meeting with a witch tomorrow. Sadie had high hopes for this meeting and would do whatever it took to prove to Astrid she could trust Sadie and fight by her side. Even if only to defeat Zagan.

CHAPTER TWENTY

SADIE

*S*adie was nervous. But it was nervous excitement. She wasn't sure if she ever had stumbled upon a witch or warlock before, but she was about to be introduced to some tonight. The men were going in human form, with hoodies covering their features so no one would recognize them. Hopefully, they would avoid any issues from arising as there was some sort of talk about mingling covens. Sadie wasn't sure. She had been too caught up in her excitement to clearly hear Damien explaining everything to Mordecai.

Kaiser and Steele stood at the door seemingly unhappy about them having to stay back and accept the allies that were set to arrive while they were gone topside. She shook her head and laughed.

"Smile, or your face will crack." She grinned at the both of them.

They faked their best smile, which she decided to ignore and gave them each a hug and kiss.

"Behave yourselves. No parties," she said to Steele.

"It wouldn't be a party without you," he said and winked.

She giggled. "Wish us luck."

Damien opened the door to the fortress and waited for Sadie and Mordecai to walk through first.

They made it about halfway through the gate when Damien paused and faced Sadie. He joined hands with her and Mordecai. And that awful sensation of being pulled came over her. Her feet left the ground, and the world around her blurred and faded to black.

Her feet settled on the ground, and she was surprised that each time she traveled like that, the nausea decreased more and more. She barely had a hint of it now.

She looked around her, instantly recognizing the heart of Seattle's downtown district. They landed here as it was supposedly closest to the underground covens, where they hoped to find Astrid.

"You ready?" Damien asked.

Sadie smiled and nodded excitedly, she forced herself to not bounce in place like a kid on Christmas morning. "Yes."

Mordecai and Damien chuckled at her response

and they headed southwest, toward the main business district, and then toward an alley between two tall buildings. Both of the princes walked closer to Sadie.

As they entered, Sadie saw a shift in the image of the two buildings. On the outside, the alley was dark, abandoned, and void of any life. On the inside, there were stalls, shops, venders, and many, many people. Chatter filled the air and there were unique smells that Sadie couldn't recognize. Some of them were sweet, while others were rotten and pungent. It was like walking through an oily substance.

"This place is hidden?" she asked.

"Yes," Damien said. "We just walked through a ward, which is slightly different than the barrier surrounding your fortress. This is meant to glamour or hide the location from anyone not meant to see this place."

"Gotcha." She took in the shops that lined both sides of the alley. Tables were set up with various items, and creatures she could only guess at sat in cages. The first one had jewelry made from teeth, bone, metal, and gems.

Sadie reached out to touch one. Mordecai caught her hand and shook his head slowly. "That is a bad idea."

"Why?" she asked.

"They're cursed," he said plainly.

She set her eyes on them again, drawn to touch them but resisting the urge. "Oh."

Witches and warlocks filtered from table to table and shop to shop. Luckily, Sadie hadn't recognized anyone yet.

"These are the witches that have devoted themselves to demons," Damien whispered loud enough for Sadie to hear but not enough for his words to carry. "They are evildoers who thrive on the torture and punishment of others, particularly humans naive enough to believe magic will benefit them in some way."

A man rushed from a shop with a sign above it that said, "Darker Intentions." His eyes were wild, but lifeless. He paused in the center of the alley just in front of them. He squeezed his eyes closed a few times and shook his head.

Sadie wondered what had happened to him. If he was human.

The man turned his attention to Sadie and a light of recognition flashed through him. He smiled, but then that slowly faded into a frown, and he seemed extremely disappointed and disoriented as he ambled aimlessly back and forth a few steps before finding his exit out of the alley.

"What was wrong with him?" she asked.

"He probably had a spell to forget placed on him." Damien shook his head. "Witches can take parts of his soul during the time the spell is being placed on him. He may have only wanted one memory taken, but greed probably caused the spell to go too far."

Sadie frowned. This was not the idea she had in mind when she thought of witches being added to her army. Hobson's words came to mind, and she vowed to keep her eyes wide opened as she learned about the witches.

"In reality, the humans are sacrificing parts of their souls. It becomes like a drug addiction. Once that small part of their soul is missing, they crave more of the magic, sacrificing pieces of their soul until there is nothing left."

A gypsy-like woman watched them from a perch on the wall between table shops and smiled at Sadie when she looked at her. The woman was young and alluring. She beckoned to Sadie with the bend of her finger. She wanted to go over to her, but Mordecai stopped her.

"What?" she asked. "I just wanna see something."

"Trust me," he said, "you don't want what she has to show you."

Sadie gave the gypsy woman another glance and the woman had the look of daggers in her eyes. Her form shifted, youthful skin peeling off and disappearing into the air and leaving older, scarred, ashen skin instead. She decided it was a good thing she had two of her men with her. Knowing too little about this world probably would've left her in a state similar to that man with the memory spell.

She saw others giving their own blood, looking worse for the wear while the witch seemed to gain more youth and smoother appearance from the life they drew from the unfortunate souls.

"That's horrible," Sadie said.

Damien shrugged. "It's how they give souls to their demon, gaining more power for him or her as well."

"Let's keep moving," Mordecai said under his breath, but she still heard him and looked back at him to make sure he was okay. His eyebrows were knitted together, and his lips formed a thin line as his eyes darted between clusters of people.

"Are you lost? Do you need help?" one witch asked from the shadows. She approached them. Her eyes settled on Sadie, and she smiled as shadows shifted through her skin and her eyes darkened, the whites taking on a glow.

Damien pulled Sadie closer to him and ignored her. Mordecai muttered under his breath something about hurrying up and finding this witch, so they could get the hell out of there.

Farther down, chains rattled against the brick. Cries for help and pleas to be released echoed toward her. Her gaze swept the crowded area as she took in the world she never had the chance to see. The world of witches bound to demons. The uncomfortable balance she needed to walk to defeat Zagan. As she drew closer, the bare feet and legs of a woman came into view. She had a tattered dress that must have once been beautiful but was dingy, stained, and full of holes now.

The woman settled her gaze on Sadie. "You can see me? Oh, thank God. Please, help. Before she returns. Please, release me."

Sadie stopped and stared at the woman. She wanted to go help her. But Damien's voice said something about being unsafe. A trick. She couldn't tell. The woman's voice took over in her head, and she couldn't focus on anything but trying to help the poor woman.

"Sadie," Damien said, stepping in front of her.

She blinked away the trance she was under and searched his eyes, wondering what was going on. "I need to help her."

He shook his head. "It's a trick meant to trap you. You are still human, and these tricks and games are aimed at fooling humans into slavery or worse."

"Please, don't listen to him. I'm real!"

Sadie tried to side-step Damien. He caught hold of her arm.

"Trust me," he said.

She switched her gaze from him to Mordecai, who nodded, hands clenched into fists at his side. She risked a final glance at the woman. She was gone, but the witch that had conjured the spell stood to the side, glaring at her and the princes.

Some of the witches Sadie had made eye contact with scowled at her, and she forced back a chill that crept up her spine. Another sensation tingled through her and she felt pulled to walk toward one of the other witches.

"Fight it, Sadie," Mordecai said.

She did. And as soon as they were past whoever tried to lure her, the feeling ebbed and she felt a rush of relief flow through her.

That made her seriously question the use of witches in her forces and she hoped the good ones were a far cry from where she currently was. Else, she would decline allies. And she couldn't afford to do that.

"Geeze," she said. "No wonder I got strange calls when I worked as a paramedic. I can see how some of these witches had caused them."

Mordecai snorted. "You haven't seen it all yet. There are rituals that turn people inside out, spells to turn clay into flesh for the grieving mothers, bloodletting that becomes a euphoric experience for the human while they are bled out and turned into decaying soldiers for their demons."

"And it gets worse from there," Damien said.

Sadie couldn't imagine the visuals that their words attempted to form in her mind. She would've emptied her stomach contents right there in the alley, which the witches probably would've used to manipulate or gain some sort of control over her. It made her queasy to think about the dark uses these witches had for naïve humans. Good thing Astrid wasn't aligned with a demon. She had no evil whims or obligations to fulfill. And that made her even more likable.

They made another series of turns, and the shops and tables ended. The number of witches tricking humans out of their souls grew less and less until they were alone, walking dark alleys toward wherever they were heading. Sadie hoped a place with a much better view. Damien and Mordecai gave her a little more breathing room as well, which she took as a good sign that the darker witches were behind them.

She was glad Astrid wasn't a part of the group they had come to first. She had seen and experienced enough evil that she was well aware that those witches would go to any lengths, including betraying their own masters, to gain whatever they desired. She couldn't afford to have that on her side.

From now on, she needed to be extremely careful of who she allowed in her fortress. Though she trusted her men and their choice of allies, she needed to be sure for herself that any ally would remain loyal and obey her and her princes, regardless of whatever prize they had their eyes set on.

With that, she hoped that the good ones were

better suited for her fight, and she knew her men would never do anything to put her in danger.

"Please tell me the next area we go to is a lot better," she said as she sighed and shook off the remaining chills that clutched her.

"Yes," Damien said while Mordecai said, "Finally."

She looked to him, he still had that determined, lost-in-thought expression.

CHAPTER TWENTY-ONE

STEELE

*S*teele stood outside the gates of the fortress and prepared for summoning his allies, the succubi. He hadn't quite figured out how to break it to them that he wouldn't have sex with them. He wasn't sure any other payment would suit them, considering how much they enjoyed having sex with him. The power boost they gained from fucking him alone was worth more to them than treasures, though he has seen it happen before. Well, not firsthand.

He sighed. *Time to get this over with.*

He reached out with his mind and found the queen. He summoned her. She responded with excitement and eagerness.

Already, this was going to be difficult. It had been too long since he had visited them last.

The succubus queen, Deseree, appeared first,

wearing her golden halter with the center cut out to expose her cleavage. Thin strips of fabric hung from her waist, covering only her butt and crotch, and she sauntered toward him, swaying her bare hips from side to side. Her long, blonde hair was pulled back to the center of her head. "Steele, how wonderful for you to stop by." She stopped right in front of him and draped her arms around his shoulders. "It's been too long. You left so quickly last time." She added a pout.

He gently removed her arms from his shoulders and said, "It has been a while. You look good."

About fifteen more succubi appeared next, and she shifted her attention to them and smiled as she rested a hand on his side. "You look as delicious as ever." She glanced behind him. "Where are we? Acquired a new fortress, I see."

"It's not mine," he said and removed her hand. He took a step back to prove his point further.

She shrugged. "We can still break in the rooms, can't we?"

A few more succubi joined Deseree on either side of him, they touched and rubbed him in all the right places. They nibbled at his ears and one sucked on his lower lip. His pants tightened, and he closed his eyes, conjuring an image of Sadie. He bit the inside of his cheek. Removing each of the succubi took time and care, and he managed to unravel himself from each of them.

"Follow me," he said and turned toward the gate.

It opened and let them through. He ignored them as they spoke about how much they missed him and couldn't wait to be with him again. It had been too long. He sighed. If he kept Sadie's face in mind, maybe that would help him stay out of trouble.

Once inside the foyer of the fortress, the succubi swarmed him again, touching, moaning, nibbling.

"Stop," he said and pulled away again.

Deseree narrowed her green eyes on him. "Why won't you have sex with us. This isn't like you, Steele." She closed the gap between them.

He took another step back. "Because Sadie, the queen of demons, asked that I invite you here. And I'm in love with her."

She pouted as her eyes darkened. "But you love having sex with us."

"Yes, that is true, as is part of my nature. But I won't be with anyone else but her now," he said.

Deseree didn't accept that as she once again closed the gap between them and grabbed his crotch and kissed on his neck.

Steele growled and pushed her away. "No." His voice was strong, firm, and left little room for argument. He stepped back. "Follow me to your rooms."

He ignored the wounded expressions and pouts as he turned around.

He headed down the hall and climbed the stairs

that led to the west wing where the guest quarters were. He figured that would suit their tastes better than the barracks. Though, he considered placing them there anyway.

He couldn't really blame them though. It was in their nature just as much as it was in his.

Once he arrived at the door, he opened it and stepped inside, keeping the door wide to allow the succubi in.

"This room is connected with three separate bedrooms off to the right there," he pointed. "You should be more than comfortable here."

Deseree sighed. "It will have to do." She turned to face him. "How about you stay for just a while longer. Perhaps I can persuade you to change your mind."

"No. I appreciate the offer, but I will not sleep with any of you."

She pouted and crossed her arms over her chest. "Fine. But I know you, Steele. You will give in. I know you will. It's only a matter of time."

He let out a frustrated sigh and said, "You are to stay here. If you need anything, Hobson will tend to your needs."

"Everyone has their limits, Steele," she said, ignoring him. "We will find your limit, break through it, and make you see the error in denying your very nature and us."

"Be prepared for endless disappointment. I had you

come here for a reason. I need you to fight alongside Sadie and me in the war against my father. For your services, I will give you the rarest of gems, jewels, and linens at my disposal." He paused, pursed his eyebrows, and held up a finger. "Wasn't it you that always complained about the south side of your castle lacking in the proper warding gems to keep it secure? You'll have several. You also needed some for your crown, as I recall. You'll have one that will allow you to cast scrying spells across great distances."

A greedy glint lit up their eyes, and he knew they were willing to forsake sex with him for the fight at least. Forever was a different question.

"You see? There is always a reason to stay loyal to me. But there is a catch."

They stood straighter, giving him their full attention.

"You will obey me and Sadie no matter what."

Deseree shook her head with a sarcastic chuckle floating through her lips. "Anything else?"

"You will not leave this room unless you are called upon by me."

"Absolutely," she said.

He leveled his gaze on her and shifted his sights to the other succubi. He knew what they were doing, and he wasn't having it. "Do not get your hopes up on me giving in to your invitations to your beds. It will never happen."

She held her head higher, a cunning smile pulled on her lips. "Of course. As long as you hold up your end of the bargain, we'll do the same."

He wanted to dig deeper into those words. There was a deeper meaning in them, but he didn't want to devote any more time in their company trying to figure it out. They were playing a game with him. Trying to strip away his will little by little. Instead, he shook his head and left them to their own devices. He needed a bit of fresh air. He could check the barrier as he did so. And that was what he headed out to do.

~

STEELE

His mind remained on Sadie. He was surprised in the changes he had undergone since she came into his life. Being able to deny the succubi hadn't been a thing for him. Not until Sadie. Though he couldn't sleep with anyone but Sadie, he still found the succubi incredibly hot. He needed—no, craved—his woman in a way he never felt before. If he didn't have her soon, he just might lose his mind. Still, he was willing to wait as long as necessary. She was worth the wait.

The absence affected him in ways he never understood, and he couldn't wait to have her back in his presence, his sight, his arms. He loved her. He was always at peace when with her. She didn't seem to mind his quirks and his lighthearted manner. She didn't judge him, and he trusted her. He was safe with her and she with him. With her, he was home.

Without her, however, he was lost. Ambling in a senseless direction.

He hoped she would be home soon. The absence of her smile and laugh, even her sexy glares she believed would be deterrents for his behaviors were evident everywhere he looked. Especially in him. She held a piece of his soul. A piece he only noticed was missing when she was gone.

"Brother," Kaiser said, walking up behind him. "You're sulking a bit much lately."

"Shouldn't you be keeping an eye on the witches?" he asked, walking with his hands in his pockets.

"Hobson, albeit unhappily, has that covered for right now. He's helping them set up a training course. I came out here to check the fortifications. Scout for places to set up guards."

Steele nodded. "Make sure to set up one outside of the succubi's rooms and at my room as well. In fact, don't. I'll just ward my door."

Kaiser chuckled. "Wow. Really? Look at what our girl has done to you. Never thought I would see the day."

"You could always go in my place," he said, giving a sideways glance and mischievous smile to his brother.

"I don't have a death wish, but thank you for the offer. I never knew you cared so much."

Steele shrugged. "It's horrible, isn't it?"

"Nah, just fooling around." Kaiser slapped Steele on the shoulder.

"Not that. Sadie being gone. You feel that too, don't you?" he asked and stopped walking to face his brother straight on.

Kaiser nodded, his expression turned serious. "I mean, how long is it supposed to take to find one witch?"

"Right?" Steele continued to walk. "Who is set to arrive next?"

"I have no idea," Kaiser said. "I think all we're waiting for now is the warlocks and witch."

Steele nodded. He thought the fortress was crowded enough sharing it with his four brothers. He didn't want to know what living arrangements would be like to have a small army of allies on top of everyone else. He shook his head. "We should set up watches for the allies. Make sure they get along."

"I'll take the first one. You look like you could use the rest."

No. What he needed was Sadie home, yesterday. But he tried to be as patient as he could with her absence. Maybe he could take some of his frustrations out on some training and extra rest. She would have to come home sooner rather than later.

At least, he hoped.

"Alright. I'll take next. Have Hobson come get me when your turn is over."

Kaiser nodded. "Sleep well, brother." He held his hand out.

Steele stared at it for a moment, as though legs or wings would sprout from the skin... it had been so long since they shared in that notion. Finally, he gripped his brother's forearm and gave a slight squeeze. He nodded.

Kaiser did the same.

He left his brother to the remainder of the perimeter check and headed for the courtyard Sadie loved to train in.

CHAPTER TWENTY-TWO

SADIE

"*S*ee all the animals?" Damien asked. "We're close."

Sadie wasn't sure what the sight of animals had to do with Astrid and said, "If you say so."

Mordecai breathed out, "Finally."

A number of animals scurried the edges of walls along the alleyway leading to a small door of what looked like an abandoned warehouse. There was a small, yellow-orange light at the side of the door that flickered dim light, barely illuminating a small circle around the door.

"Every time I've seen Astrid, she's been surrounded by animals. I learned she has an affinity for them and uses her powers to heal and take care of them."

Mordecai searched the shadows and muttered, "We need to hurry this up."

"This is it," Damien said, pointing to the door with the flickering light.

Mordecai sighed, and continued to search the shadows for whatever it was that set him on edge. But Sadie wondered if it wasn't just the situation. Witches were the counterparts of warlocks. Maybe there was something wrong with him hanging out with witches as well? Either way, he was definitely on edge and that made her want to know why.

She was about to ask when a thin woman with long dark hair stepped out of the door with a bag full of kibble. She scattered the food in front of the door and all the animals scurried to catch their little piece of sustenance. The little chitters and squeaks made her giggle. Sadie wondered if that was her.

Damien stopped walking and said, "She has a strong ability to heal. She can take care of almost any ailment known to man and a few unknown. She's a strong warrior in magic of light and is very capable to hold her own in battle."

Sadie nodded and turned her attention back to the woman. "So that's her?"

He nodded.

"Damien?" Astrid said. "Is that you?"

He smiled and approached. "Yes. I'm sorry for arriving unannounced, but I'm afraid we have urgent need of your services."

She pursed her eyebrows. "How so? Who is with you?"

He gestured to Sadie and his brother and said, "This is Sadie, the new demon queen, and my brother Mordecai. Please don't say anything about her. We're trying to lie low with my father on the loose. We came to call in a few favors."

She nodded. "And I'm one favor you're calling in." It came out more like a statement than a question, and Sadie noticed that the witch was instantly wary and suspicious of her and Mordecai.

"Yes." Damien stopped at the border of the ring of light surrounding the door.

"I have no reason to ally with any *demon*," she looked to Sadie, "or demon queen. How are you human?" She turned her gaze back to Damien. "How do I know what you said is true?"

"I have had no reason to lie to you before, and I don't now," Damien said.

She shifted her attention back to Sadie. "I want proof."

Whether it was the fact that she accused Damien of lying to her or that she was forced to prove herself to a witch, Sadie was annoyed by constantly being questioned of her human nature and being demon queen at the same time. Still, she could see that Astrid was guarded and hesitant to even discuss the possibility of helping.

"Zagan is on a warpath to ultimate domination. I currently stand in his way. He's threatened by my power, and his is growing. How much longer do you think you can realistically refuse him? If I fall into his hands, Zagan will be unstoppable. You won't be able to resist him. I would be honored to have your aid in preventing him from taking over the underworld entirely. Please, join us. Help us end his reign."

Astrid seemed to think over things a little but didn't seem to sway toward her.

Mordecai shifted his weight and searched the dark alley nearby. Sadie wondered what he kept looking for. But before she could ask him about it, Damien spoke again, pulling her attention back to the conversation.

"Astrid," Damien said. "All we're asking for is some help."

She snorted. "Yeah, and then comes the high-pressure sales for my soul. No thanks."

"I would be honored if you agreed to help," Sadie said. "And there will be no binding yourself to me or any demon for your help. I promise."

"No offense," Astrid said, "But I don't take the word of demons or their queens. I've been there, done that and not happening."

Sadie's hope diminished slightly. Still, she wasn't willing to give up just yet. There had to be a way to get Astrid on her side.

Soft whimpering echoed to her from the farthest part of the alley. Sadie focused her eyes and senses. There was a small puppy, all alone and sounding hurt. Her heart hurt for the poor thing and her natural need to take care of it kicked in.

She made her way to the little guy, picked him up, and cradled him close to her body as she noticed that he was bleeding badly. Someone or something had done this to him. She cradled him close to her body and carried him to Astrid.

"He needs help," she said to Astrid. "He's covered in blood."

Astrid seemed taken aback. "I've never expected a caring and giving heart from a demon queen." She held her arms out for the puppy and Sadie carefully passed him over. Astrid nodded. "Follow me."

She glanced back at the men who nodded at her. She followed the witch inside. As she stepped in, she was shocked that the building on the inside looked well maintained with clean, white walls and sterling silver equipment.

Astrid stepped into a room off to the right and Sadie followed. The witch set the puppy on the exam table and began shifting through his fur for the sources of the wound. Her eyes closed, and she tilted her head up. Her hands hovered over the puppy, and the whimpering slowed to a stop as the wounds sealed right in front of Sadie's eyes.

"Grab the formula behind you," Astrid said.

Sadie nodded and turned around to find a set of bottles and cans of puppy formula sitting on the counter. She pulled the tab off one of the cans, filled a bottle, and twisted on the nipple. Turning, she held the tip of the bottle so that some of the liquid would drip in front of the puppy and he sniffed it and found the nipple, sucking as though the poor thing hadn't eaten in weeks.

"That was amazing, what you did there," Sadie said.

"Thanks. I'll be right back." She left the room and returned a few minutes later with a vet-tech. "Keep an eye on him and make sure he stays warm and is able to pass the food easily. Alert me if there are any complications."

The tech nodded and took over feeding the puppy.

She followed Astrid back out. The witch stood in front of Damien with her hands crossed and most of her weight on one leg. She seemed to think over a few things in her head and shifted her eyes to Sadie.

"Zagan, huh?" she asked.

Sadie nodded.

With a sigh, she stood straighter and said, "I'll help, but I refuse to pledge myself to any demon. I have made it thus far and don't want to commit myself to anyone. I enjoy being free and don't want to feel like I'm at the beck and call of any demon who may end up using me for nefarious means and eventually own my soul. I refuse to never get the rest I deserve once my life on this realm is over."

"That may not last much longer," Damien said. "Surely you've seen the signs that my father's power has accelerated and continues to do so. We both know that you, and the coven you protect, don't have much longer before bonding with a demon will provide more protection for you. Sadie would be your best option."

"She's human."

He shook his head. "Not entirely."

Sadie blushed a little internally. It was sweet that he wanted Astrid to pledge loyalty to her. Though she wasn't sure about how that happened. Maybe they could figure out a different way if it came down to it. Right now, she was just so relieved that Astrid agreed to help them. That was a check in the victory box. And that was enough for Sadie.

Astrid went silent as she thought about Damien's words. Finally, she said, "It would take someone seriously special for me to align myself with a demon. However, I don't trust Zagan either. I know time is running out, but I won't be rushed into anything. Especially not something so important. Not with so many lives hanging on my choice."

Sadie wondered what she meant by that. What

lives would hang in the balance due to Astrid's decision on aligning herself with her? Maybe she knew of a war bigger than hers and Zagan's? Or perhaps her coven was a lot larger than anyone realized.

She silently considered the possibilities, not yet trusting Astrid enough to show all her cards.

Astrid turned to Sadie. "I will help, but I promise nothing. I will spend time with you and determine for myself if we're… compatible. If this works out, perhaps I can convince my coven sisters and warlocks to join you as well.

"How many have you accumulated now?" Damien asked, arms crossed over his chest.

Mordecai had taken to holding up the side of the building with a foot resting on the side and his arms also crossed over his chest. He stared into the dark alley still, just as on edge as before.

She smiled. "More than one hundred. That's all I'll divulge."

"What exactly will you be looking for when it comes to spending time with me?" Sadie asked.

Astrid shrugged. "I want to see who you really are. If the kindness is just a perceived front. After all, demon queens aren't exactly noted for their kind histories and reputations."

Sadie forced back a laugh, deciding just to go along with the flow of everything. She really should be used to people not trusting her.

"We'll send word to your coven once we're back at the fortress. When you are ready to send for them, we'll do so at once. We've been gone for too long, and we need to return immediately."

CHAPTER TWENTY-THREE

SADIE

*T*hey started to walk out of the alley when Sadie's amulet warmed with a warning. She focused on the sensation, hoping to decipher what it meant. There was still so much about her amulet's magic that she didn't understand.

The air shifted, turning colder than before and filling with tension.

The streets seemed quieter. A sense of being watched overcame Sadie. She looked to Damien and Mordecai. Both seemed on edge and watched the shadows while Astrid maintained her composure. Her eyes darted through the area around them.

The shadows in front of them moved. The group stopped and moved in close.

"Shit," Damien said.

Mordecai summoned his smoke staff and said, "Father's envoy."

A man led the group of eight demons. Each of them armed to the teeth and looking ready for a fight. The leader's eyes focused on Astrid, and a wicked smile stretched across his face. "My master wishes to have an audience with you and requests," he chuckled and looked to his demon backup, "that you join him."

Requests my ass. Sadie wasn't about to let Astrid go without a fight. Even with a fight. Zagan could go to hell.

Astrid stood a little taller and firmly said, "Tell your *master* that I must decline his offer."

The demons joined in with the leader's chuckle. He settled his dark, threatening gaze on the witch and said, "I was so hoping you'd say that."

He threw a ball of fire at Astrid. Sadie jumped in front of her, summoned her smoke wall, and blocked the flaming missile before the heat could even warm the air. She summoned her shadow sword and looked to Astrid. "You all right?" she asked.

Astrid nodded. She had a look of surprise and gratitude. But that assessment would have to wait. Sadie had to teach these assholes a lesson for picking on the wrong people.

The man smiled, eyes glowing green, and signaled to the shadows on either side of them.

A group of witches and warlocks flanked them on each side, charging at full-speed. Damien and Mordecai held them off, each taking a side. Meanwhile, Sadie took on the leader and his demon groupies with Astrid at her side.

The man leading the group came first and Sadie rushed in to meet him, swinging her sword down on him. He blocked it with the vambrace that covered his forearm. He absorbed the shock and turned the metal from silver to black. He took his gloved hand and shoved it forward, fingers splayed out. The glove glowed blue and a force hit Sadie, tossing her back. Her sword fell from her hands and disappeared.

Sadie realized the man she was fighting was a warlock. He didn't use magic in the way she understood witches did but used magic-infused armor instead. She needed to quickly think of a way to take care of him before all their work in getting Astrid was thrown away.

The warlock wasted no time in trying to grip Astrid's arm. She twisted to the side and elbowed him in the back. Sadie quickly climbed to her feet and rushed to Astrid's side as four of the demons approached from behind, the other four charging from the front.

Sadie conjured the magic in her amulet, needing to take demons out immediately. The warlock came up from behind her as her amulet warmed and pulsed through her body. Her hands warmed and took on the glow of purple and dark blue. The warlock's arms wrapped around her body and she headbutted him in the face. But he didn't let go.

He chuckled darkly in her ear. "It'll take a lot more than that for you to best me."

She nodded. "Okay."

She stomped his foot and placed her hands on his sides. A bright blast of light flashed, and the warlock screamed. She turned, hoping to find him in nothing but a pile of ash, but instead stood there with burning, charred holes in his sides.

He panted. "Bitch! You'll pay for that."

"Not yet." She turned and conjured her shield and sword of fire. She shot a blast of fire at the demon that had a hold of Astrid's arm. She struggled to free herself from its grip but it was useless. She was on the verge of ripping her arm off with the hold the demon had on her limb.

Sadie took a step forward to slice the demon's arm off, but Astrid's eyes turned white and a bolt of lightning shot straight into the top of his head from the sky. He limply fell to the ground as smoke poured from the crater in his skull like a chimney. Sadie nodded in approval and lunged forward as she was kicked in the back. She caught herself from hitting the ground and turned on her heels to jab her sword at the warlock.

He blocked the move again with his vambrace and she used the sword to block his hand from the same move he made before and kicked him in his gut. She jumped into the air, sword high, and as she landed, sliced through his armor. He stumbled backward, dazed from the blows, and she thrust her sword forward, sinking her flaming blade into the warlock's abdomen. He screamed as he burst into flames and fell to the ground in a heaping pile of burning flesh.

Sadie turned in time to see Astrid using the roots of the trees nearby to hold the other six demons in place while she dodged every blow and grip of the seventh. She quickly checked on her men, finding they were also making progress in their fight. Mordecai kept phasing through the shadows and catching his opponents from behind while Damien expertly used Lightbane to dispatch his attackers, dodging each magical attack thrown at him.

Satisfied, Sadie rushed to take care of the other demon. She was impressed Astrid could handle herself for the most part. Obviously, her skills were limited in concentration. Proving Sadie's assessment, the toe of Astrid's shoe caught on a lifted edge of cement and she crumbled to the ground. The roots loosened around the other demon's legs and the seventh one lunged for her.

Sadie shot a ball of fire toward the seventh demon and ran for the other six trying to free themselves from the roots.

The shot landed in the seventh demon's shoulder, distracting him enough to give Astrid time to stand and regain her concentration.

"You maintain the roots. I'll take care of the rest," Sadie said.

Astrid nodded, and her eyes became white again.

Sadie faced off with the demon, his black eyes narrowed in on her.

"So, this is the new demon queen?" He spat at the ground near her feet. "You'll never be *my* queen. You're just a human woman playing at a role you're unworthy of. Zagan will destroy you."

Sadie shrugged. "Suit yourself." She attacked, and he dodged, shooting black streams of smoke at her. The streams sharpened into blades as they neared her. She tried to dodge them the best she could, but some managed to cut her on the arm and her cheek.

"Pathetic human." He shook his head as he paced a circle around her. "You deserve what's coming to you."

She pursed her eyebrows and wondered what the hell he meant by that. As she caught her breath and kept an eye on the demon circling her, she realized that each attack to them was only meant to disarm, not kill. Her and the demon princes were the ones killing. Even Astrid held the offensive stance as she merely aimed to keep herself from being captured.

The realization of Zagan having the same idea for Astrid hit her. That had to be the reason. He wanted the witch's powers in the fight against her and her men.

That motherfucker.

"Enough!" Sadie's voice carried through the night, stilling the fight. She looked around as everyone looked to her. Her amulet cast a faint red glow around her, and she pointedly glared at the remainder of the attacking group. "This fight ends now, or you will all die. Go back and tell your master that he was too late in getting the witch on his side. Next time I see him, he will die."

The seventh demon snorted. "Or you'll what? Talk us to death?"

That was the last straw. She shoved her sword into the demon's gut and used the power in her amulet to turn him into ash. As the little charred pieces of him fell, she turned to face what was left of everyone. "Anyone else care to say another smart-ass remark?" She settled her eyes on the witches. "Unless you are itching to be a slave to your master for the rest of eternity, I suggest you take what life you have left and leave."

Damien and Mordecai joined Sadie and Astrid. The witches slowly turned and disappeared into the dark shadows between buildings and trees. Sadie turned her attention to the demons bound by tree roots.

"Release them," she said to Astrid.

The roots untwisted and returned to the earth. The demons shook off their legs and feet and narrowed their eyes on Sadie and her group.

One of the demons pointed at her. "We'll be back. This isn't the last you've seen of us."

Sadie rolled her eyes. "Fabulous, you bring the drinks and I'll bring the cake."

They turned and headed the same direction they came from. Once they were out of sight, Sadie turned to Astrid and asked, "Are you all right?"

She nodded. "I'm fine. Thank you. You really must be a force to reckon with if Zagan sent a convoy for me this time."

"This time?" Damien asked.

"Yeah, he's never really stopped trying to get me. I think tonight just goes to prove he's desperate. He's a big reason why I won't give loyalty to any demon."

"You should've said something before now."

"Why? We have a loose friendship at best, Damien. And you're still a demon. Human form or not."

Sadie took inventory of her men and Astrid while her and Damien talked. Everyone seemed to have endured minor cuts and scrapes and singed clothing. Overall, everyone was relatively unhurt. Relief flooded her. She would've hated for one of her men, or Astrid, to have been seriously injured. She was so grateful everyone was fine.

"Then you agree," Mordecai asked. "Zagan must be defeated."

She sighed. "I hate Zagan. The majority of us do. Regardless, he's a problem and a threat to the balance. He needs to be defeated." She casted a wary gaze toward Sadie. "No one should have that much power."

"We're working on finding a way right now," Damien said. "You were step one in that process."

She nodded, took in a deep breath, and hesitated for a moment. She seemed to have been working through the pros and cons of something. She flicked her gaze to Sadie again and a wrinkle appeared in the center of her forehead.

Sadie wondered if she was still trying to decide if she could be trusted. After what she had just done to make sure the witch stayed alive, she hoped she was heading in the right direction. Otherwise, what was the point of going through so much effort?

"Well, I have heard of one way we could defeat him. It's not a guarantee though."

"Let's hear it," Sadie said. "I'm willing to try anything to keep him from taking over."

"There's a book. An ancient tome closely guarded by dangerous creatures not even I can tame. It's the forbidden book, full of knowledge and lore on demons. A charm was placed on it so that it could never be destroyed and only a powerful witch can read it."

"I'm guessing there is a catch to this wonderous book of yours," Mordecai said.

She nodded. "Only a demon can enter, and any witch who has ever tried to get the book has been killed."

"So, if I'm understanding this correctly," Sadie said. "There is a book that explains how to kill demons, that only a demon can take, but also only a witch can read?"

"Essentially, yes," Astrid said. "Again, it's not a guarantee. And let's not forget I could die for trying."

Sadie didn't like the idea. But right now, it was their only shot at defeating Zagan for good. She looked at Damien and Mordecai. They didn't seem too thrilled with the idea as well, but nodded.

They were on board. Astrid was on board.

Mordecai said, "I know of the book she refers to. It exists, but it's been locked away for a reason. Even Zagan has tried and failed to take it for himself."

"We've beat him once already. I think we could handle this challenge too. Are you sure you are willing to risk your life for this book?" Sadie asked.

"Yes. I wouldn't have offered otherwise." Astrid shook her head.

Sadie still wasn't convinced this was a good idea,

but it was their only option so far. She needed to give it a real shot. If Astrid was truly willing to give her life to help her and her men with defeating the demon king, she needed to take that opportunity and hope that Astrid survived.

"Let's go then," Sadie said, gesturing for Astrid to lead the way.

CHAPTER TWENTY-FOUR

KAISER

*K*aiser sat in a plush chair in his room. He shifted so that he was in proper position and closed his eyes. He reached out through his mental connection with the queen of gorgons. The lights flickered in his room, creating dark flashes through his lids. The connection was created.

"Yes, my dear prince?" the queen said.

"I have need of you and your strongest warriors. Come to the fortress in Bitterthorn at once." He pushed as much urgency as he could muster into his mental words.

But there was hesitation from the queen, which he had not counted on. Normally, he would ask, and she delivered. No questions asked. He wondered what the change was and worried she would deny him. He hadn't counted on his allies refusing him. He would hate to force them.

"Is there something wrong?" she asked.

"I need you with a fight against my father."

A sensation prickled through him similar to excitement but with a hunger for blood and death. Goosebumps broke out along his skin, and that told him all he needed to know. Not only was the queen willing to come to his aid, she craved the fight.

"I'll bring my finest warriors. Look for our arrival within the day." Her voice was colored with the same excitement that still coursed along Kaiser's skin.

He sighed. "As always, looking forward to another battle alongside you."

He broke the connection and opened his eyes. The sudden stillness and emptiness of the room stared at him. The lack of Sadie's presence was noted in every nook and cranny. Damn, he missed her and couldn't wait for the chance to have her back in his arms again.

He used his connection to her through the charm he had placed in her lower back to check on her several times while she was gone. He did so again, finding her on her way back to the underworld. He sighed with relief. It wouldn't be much longer until he would get his wish of her in his arms.

His stomach growled loudly. He had been so consumed with the lack of his woman's presence and calling on his allies that he had completely forgotten to eat. All day long. He shook his head as he stood from his chair and made his way to the door. But as he reached for the handle, a sensation prickled through him. It was Sadie. There was trouble. He itched to jump up and run to her rescue, but he knew his brothers were there and wouldn't let anything happen to her.

There were a few slices of pain and Kaiser hissed as he stood at the door, hands clenched to his sides. She was in trouble, and every instinct within him told him to run to her and help.

But he couldn't leave. He could always find her, sure, but if he left now, he would be leaving Steele to his own devices and that would never do.

Dammit.

He paced the room, continuing to feel the pain that rushed through Sadie's body at whatever trouble they had come across.

Of course, he knew that there was a possibility of something happening while she was gone. He trusted his brothers enough to protect her and keep her well. Not to mention she was perfectly capable of taking care of herself. He had seen that a number of times since he first met her.

Calm down.

He worked on taking in slow breaths and releasing them. Before he knew it, the pain had stopped, and elation took its place.

See. Nothing to worry about. All handled.

He nodded to himself and continued his mission to the kitchen. He had a mad hankering for some roasted chicken that was left over from the day before. His stomach rumbled in agreement. He laughed to himself.

Worried for nothing.

CHAPTER TWENTY-FIVE

SADIE

*A*s her feet landed on the ground from exiting the portal, her knees grew weak, but she managed to stay standing.

Looking around, she saw the area was dark, decrepit, and the mountains were coated with veins of molten lava. Streams of the magma ran in rivers throughout the rocky terrain. The air was filled with sulfur, burning the back of Sadie's throat and making her eyes water.

Mordecai and Damien stood at each side of Sadie, and Astrid moved from behind her to the front as she searched for a direction to go in.

"Where are we?" Sadie asked.

Damien said, "We're in one of the deeper parts of the Void. A place where even demons wouldn't dare go. It's dangerous here, so stay alert."

Great. As if the dangers of getting the book weren't steep enough, they had managed to travel to a place where even the demon princes hesitated to tread. The information the book had was of utmost importance to their fight with Zagan. They needed that information.

"Where to?" Sadie asked.

Astrid pointed to a series of caves up ahead. Ones with strange and monstrous creatures guarding the entrances. "There."

Of course, they would have to fight on top of it all. What part of Sadie's job and success ever came without one?

"Do you know which cave exactly?" Sadie asked.

Astrid shook her head. "No. But there are two caverns that will lead to either an eternal fall into darkness, or a painful death."

This just keeps getting better and better.

"The third, and I suspect that the caverns magically change, will lead to the book and many other things that are too powerful for just anyone to hold. That's the way the angels like it."

That part really didn't surprise Sadie. She was learning that the angels had their hands in more than just Evangeline's duty to keep an eye on Sadie and her growth as demon queen. And it seemed like something they would do. Set up a series of caves to make it damn near impossible to get anything that would help them defeat Zagan.

"I can scope them out," Mordecai said.

"No," Sadie said. The last thing she wanted was him falling forever into a dark pit or dying. It was too dangerous. She wouldn't be able to live with herself if he got seriously hurt or killed, much less be lost to her forever.

He turned to face her. "I'm the only one that can skirt by undetected. I float, remember? Shadow form?"

Right. That. She sighed. "Fine. Just be careful."

He smiled. "You got it, Captain." He shifted into shadow and floated across the distance to the caves.

The three sat on the ground while they waited for Mordecai to come back. Sadie looked around at the terrain while Astrid seemed to meditate, and Damien pulled at dead pieces of grass from the cracked dirt. No one talked. That suited Sadie just fine. She wasn't one for idle chatter and this didn't seem like the place to carry on random conversations.

Finally, Mordecai returned. He was paler than before, and eyes were wide with whatever horror he had seen. He gulped. "I found it."

Sadie wanted to ask what had set him on edge so much, but she figured she would find out soon enough. They all stood and set off for the cave.

As they neared the entrance, a strange creature moved across the opening. It made rapid clicking sounds as it moved, like hooves against stone. It faced them, and Sadie gaped. The creature had the mane of a lion, the face of a goat, but the eyes of a snake. It flicked its tongue out at them as well.

"Don't look in its eyes," Damien said.

Sadie focused on how it moved.

The creature had six hooved feet in a complete diameter around it. When it moved, it rotated from hoof to hoof.

She conjured her smoke sword as they drew nearer, and the creature toppled to its side, catching itself on its legs so that it looked like a strange, furry medallion. It screeched at them and charged.

Five more came to its aid.

As it left the cave, something glimmered on its knees and Sadie realized they were sharp claws like teeth on a saw blade.

Mordecai shifted to shadow, dodging the creatures. Damien used Lightbane to hack at the ones that got too close to him. Astrid conjured boulders from the ground to block their path, forcing them to either quickly maneuver around the rocks or hit them.

Sadie tried to slice at one, but it had dodged her swing and spat fizzing green liquid at her. A drop landed on her hand and ate away at the skin. Astrid quickly rushed over, but a creature had come up from behind her. Sadie pushed her out of the way and tossed a ball of fire at it. It squeaked as it ran away, combusting into more flames until it hit the ground and stopped moving.

Mordecai shoved his staff into the mouth of the one that headed for him. It bit off a chunk of his staff as he stared at the creature with wide eyes.

Sadie shot a ball of fire at it too, but it saw the flame coming for it and rushed away.

"What the hell are these things?" Sadie asked.

"Buers, or some weird hybrid of them," Damien answered as he managed to dispatch two of the creatures at the same time. "Look out!"

Damien rushed Sadie and used Lightbane like a baseball bat to knock the creature into oblivion.

The remaining two scattered, rushing away like frightened dogs.

Sadie faced Damien and said, "Thanks."

Mordecai showed up and took Sadie's injured hand into his. "Looks like you got only enough on it to cause it to blister and eat the first few layers of skin. You'll be fine."

"How are you holding up, Astrid?" she asked, turning to face her.

"Fine," she said with a firm nod.

They headed into the mouth of the cave, following Mordecai. Sadie conjured a ball of fire in her hand to light the way. Damien kept Lightbane in his hands for additional light. Even with them lighting the darkness around them, it seemed to push back, fighting for dominance.

A chill crept over Sadie's skin and she forced back the need to shiver.

"Get ready," Mordecai whispered as they entered a larger room.

At the farthest end, just before the black swallowed it whole, stood another terrifying creature. It appeared to be sleeping and they worked to keep their steps soft and their breathing whisper quiet.

Sadie narrowed her gaze on the creature that appeared the size of a small house. It also looked like a strange spider with a torso and head like a human. Its arms and legs ended in sharp points.

She found as they drew closer, she instinctively held her breath more and more.

A rock fell from somewhere above them, waking the creature on the floor. Everyone stood still. Its eyes opened and fell on Sadie, and her heart skipped a beat. She wasn't sure whether or not to douse the flames or stand completely still.

Another creature of the same type lowered itself from the ceiling by silver threading Sadie thought was web. It dropped to the floor and let out a loud, ear-piercing scream. The other creature woke and let out its own scream as well.

Sadie released the flame in her hand and conjured her fire sword and shield. The creature shot web toward them. Everyone dashed and rolled away from the sticky strands and rushed to fight the creature.

The ground rumbled, and rocks fell around them.

"Run for the doorway!" Mordecai yelled as the ground continued to shake.

Everyone stopped what they were doing and ran for the direction Mordecai had indicated. Once they were through, the doorway sealed, and they were locked inside.

Torches lined the walls. Sadie lit one and the rest illuminated, one-by-one until the room was filled with warm light. In the center of the room, surrounded by a pool of water was a dais. The book sat on top, guarded by two large statues. One was of a demon, and the other was of an angel, locked in a frozen war.

"What happened?" Damien asked.

Astrid said, "The rooms changed."

"How do we get out?" Sadie asked.

"Portal," Mordecai said.

Sadie nodded then walked to a stone bridge that created a path between where they stood and the dais. She took a step on the walk path and was stopped by Astrid, holding her arm. She shook her head and said, "A demon has to do it."

"I'll go," Damien said and started walking across.

Sadie watched as she waited for another trap to trip with each step he took across. When he finally reached the book, he slipped it under his arm and walked back. He gave it to Sadie.

She held the strange, brown leather-bound book in her hands. There were no inscriptions on the cover or spine. She flipped open the cover and the words written on the front page became scrambled and shifted into strange symbols and swirls. She closed the cover and pressed a hand to her forehead, overcome with dizziness.

Astrid held her hands out. "Only a witch can read it, remember?"

Sadie was hesitant. She didn't know Astrid's true intentions much less sure she could trust the witch completely yet. Still, if she was their only hope at finding a way to defeat Zagan, she needed to extend the olive branch on this one.

She handed over the book.

Astrid's eyes widened with excitement and a giant smile stretched her lips as she scanned the book. She dragged a finger along the center of each page before turning to another.

"There is a weapon I have been searching for. It's a bladed staff. I wanted it for protection against Zagan and his advances as well as other demons, but I believe it would be better suited for you."

Well, that is nice of her. "I appreciate that." Sadie smiled.

"The staff is etched with magical runes and dipped and infused with a special poison."

"Poison?" Sadie asked. "Will that work?"

Astrid says, "If Zagan has too many souls in his body, then he is beyond corrupt and dangerous. The poison will wound the king and have him lose control over the souls in his body, thus weakening him for a time." She held up a finger. "But, I would have to do more research before placing belief in a staff that could solve all our problems."

Sadie nodded. "Then time is what we will give, but we can't afford much. Try your best to figure that out as soon as possible."

Astrid nodded.

"Meanwhile, let's get back," she said to her men.

Astrid tucked her book close to her chest and huddled closer to the rest of the group as the floor disappeared beneath them and a floating sensation took over.

CHAPTER TWENTY-SIX

KAISER

*K*aiser made his rounds, checking on the allies, making sure everything was still in order. A gorgon stopped him in the hall and asked, "Where might I find the dining room?"

Kaiser nodded and tried to give the instructions without confusing his ally, but it was no use. Her brow formed wrinkles and her lips turned down at the corners. The poor girl was confused. With a sigh, he resigned to showing her himself.

If he hadn't had the strength Sadie granted him, he didn't think he would be able to make it through the overwhelming experience of so many people living under one roof, never mind very different creatures and all of them potentially dangerous. The opportunities for taking over were too many to count, and

Kaiser had to remind himself to keep the faith that this was all for the good of everyone in the end.

He had felt the shift in his world the moment Sadie left. And again, the second she was back. It was like he could finally breathe again. He quickly rushed through the fortress to the foyer and wrapped her into his arms, planting kisses on her.

Sadie giggled and tried to pry herself from him. "Okay. Okay! I missed you too."

His eyes opened and settled on a woman he recognized. Instantly, he pulled from Sadie and regained his composure. She lifted her eyebrows and shifted glances between the three brothers and Sadie.

Sadie's dragon let out a call and flew into the room, landing right in front of Astrid. Pyra roared and Kaiser watched as Sadie seemed hesitant to jump in. He didn't know what to do, and it seemed she didn't know either. Her hands clenched and took on a warm glow as her magic stirred within her. Her amulet lit with swirling reds. She sighed and relaxed a bit, seemingly okay with just standing back and watching.

Astrid smiled and said, "What a magnificent beasty you are!" She petted Pyra on the snout. She whined then lowered herself to the ground at the witch's feet and allowed more petting. Astrid laughed.

Sadie let out a breath, drawing Kaiser's attention as he watched with bated breath as well. The witch and dragon seemed to bond, and Sadie seemed okay with that. She glanced at Kaiser, smiled, and turned her attention back to her dragon.

Astrid said, "Sadie, you are so lucky to have such a wonderful majestic creature at your side."

Kaiser also let out a breath, the tension left his shoulders from the potentially dangerous interaction.

But what caught Kaiser off guard the most was that, up until now, the dragon only preferred Sadie and was loyal only to her.

"Excuse me if I come off accusatory," Sadie said, "But what did you do to my dragon? Is this your affinity?"

Astrid stood and didn't seem bothered or offended by her question in the least. "Any animal can sense the type of person you are. Whether or not you have good or bad intentions. It's part of their ability to thrive and survive dangerous situations. It really doesn't have anything to do with my affinity for creatures, although that probably helps."

That was good to know. At least she didn't need to worry about Astrid stealing Pyra. Not that she was worried about that all that much. Just a little. And with that, she also wondered what Astrid could show her in terms of tricks with the hellhounds.

Steele appeared in the room. He wrapped Sadie in a huge hug.

Sadie pulled away and said, "Now that everyone is

here, allow me to introduce Astrid. Astrid, this is Steele and Kaiser, Damien's other two brothers."

She smiled and said, "Nice to meet everyone."

"There's more," Kaiser said.

Sadie narrowed her eyes on him. "What do you mean, more?"

"Allies have begun to arrive. We have witches, warlocks, gorgons, and succubi all housed and waiting for your arrival."

She nodded. "Right. Give me some time to get cleaned up and changed. I'll meet everyone in the throne room."

Kaiser nodded.

She summoned Hobson who showed within record time. "Yes, Your Highness?"

"This is Astrid. She has agreed to aid us in the war against Zagan. Please show her to her room."

"At once," he said.

"Please, treat your new quarters as your home. As long as you are here, you are home."

Astrid nodded. "I appreciate that."

She followed Hobson out of the room. Sadie excused herself to get cleaned up.

SADIE

*S*he had just climbed out of the bath and wrapped herself in a towel when she heard footsteps along the floor of her bedroom. She closed her eyes and focused on the rhythm.

Kaiser.

She smiled and shook her head as the memory of how he greeted her replayed through her mind. She stepped out of the bathroom and found Kaiser pacing her room.

"I don't think Hobson would appreciate having to resurface the floors with all your pacing. You're going to wear a path into it."

He stopped pacing and faced her. She could tell he struggled with whether or not to scoop her up again, and she smiled and winked. He seemed to relax then, chuckling under his breath and running a hand through his hair.

"What can I do for you?" she asked.

"What happened while you were gone?" he asked.

She pursed her eyebrows and narrowed her eyes on him. "What do you mean?"

He pointed to the scratches on her arms and said, "I know you guys had trouble up there. What happened. Please?"

Sadie sighed. "It was nothing we couldn't handle. Just your father trying to force Astrid into his ranks."

"But you are okay?" he asked, eyes filled with worry.

She nodded and turned so he could look her over and said, "I'm positive."

He sighed with relief. His shoulders relaxed, and he took a seat at the foot of her bed.

"If you don't mind, I need to get dressed. You need to get your allies ready."

"Right." He jumped up, approached her, and planted a kiss on her forehead before giving her a long look in her eyes. He sighed and left the room.

She shook her head. *Men. And they say women are the enigmas.*

CHAPTER TWENTY-SEVEN

SADIE

*S*adie sat on her throne, wearing a long, blood-red dress with black lace. She made sure to wear a crown to keep up the appearance and formality of meeting with the allies.

Because the allies were apprehensive being in the same room together at first, she decided it was a good idea to call on them individually. Kaiser stood at the center of the room with his band of gorgons behind him. They were humanoid with scales covering their bared skin and had collections of snakes on their heads. Their skin color varied from yellows, reds, oranges, to greens and blacks. Just like the snakes she knew about topside.

Sadie was unsure of what to think of them at first. They reminded her too much of the empusa and she wondered if they were truly loyal to Kaiser or if they somehow had connections to Hecate.

There were about twenty-five of them, each armored to the nines and as beautiful as they were imposing and terrifying in nature. They fascinated her in the way that she had never seen them before, except for Greek mythology stories she had learned about in high school. To see them standing before her was a treat, and it thrilled her that so much of what she learned as fiction was in fact, reality.

There was one gorgon that stood at the center of the group in the front row. She also had a crown, which fascinated Sadie. A queen working for a queen. Interesting.

With a deep breath, she let it out slow, deciding that she couldn't put off the demonstration any longer.

"Kaiser," she said, "you may begin."

"Sadie, queen of demons, I present to you my allies who I called upon to aid you in your war with Zagan, the king of demons, ruler of Shardford. It is my honor to introduce Her Majesty of the gorgon people, Queen Rezios."

Sadie forced back a giggle. That was way too formal for Kaiser.

He bowed at the waist and moved to the side to allow the queen of gorgons to step forward. She was impressively regal and beautiful. Her skin was silver with diamonds of black and tan along her legs and arms, and an intricate design plunged along her neck line, accenting her ample cleavage. The snakes on her head were all black and silver and wove around her crown that was made of ice.

"Greetings, queen of demons." Her voice was thick and carried an accent that made her words harsh and melodic at the same time. "I'm Rezios. My people have been hunted by Zagan for centuries. It would be an honor to fight by your side."

Sadie nodded. "Thank you. The honor is mine."

Rezios cocked her head to the side. "Forgive me, Your Highness, but I would like for you to prove that you are the demon queen. You are much different from Hecate. And human, it seems."

Sadie rolled her eyes. It was because she said thank you. She couldn't help it. That's just how she was.

Still, Sadie stood from her throne and let the amulet embedded in her chest be seen as it started to glow. Her hands warmed as she stared at the queen who came into her home and demanded proof of her power. Fire ignited from her palms and she leveled her gaze on the gorgon queen. "Satisfied? Or do you still need more proof?"

The queen took a few steps to the right and then to the left of Sadie, maintaining her distance but still inspecting the power she had emitted. Finally, she stood at the center and nodded once.

"I'm satisfied, for now. I will ask for further proof on the field of course, before my army fights."

Oh, for the love of... "Very well. Now, I must ask the same of you."

The gorgon queen lifted an eyebrow. "How so?"

"Demonstrate to me your skills. Just because you were invited here doesn't mean you are guaranteed a position in my ranks or on the field. I must know that your skills will be useful in my fight."

The queen stared blankly at Sadie for a moment before bowing her head and turning to her group. She made a few gestures, her army's eyes never wavered from her. With a unified nod, the group shifted into pairs. Some procured ice weapons and shields. What fascinated Sadie the most was the maces. Sharp spikes of ice produced from a handle.

The queen let out a noise Sadie couldn't replicate if she tried, and the pairs sparred with each other with extreme skill. What shocked her the most was as they were getting injured, red blood pooled and splattered on the marble floor of her throne room.

Sadie called for Hobson to join her side. As she watched the demonstration, the gargoyle stood to her left. "Yes, Majesty?" he asked.

"I apologize. I didn't realize they would literally try to kill themselves."

"Of course, Sadie. You asked them for a demon-stration. They don't know any other way than to show you their own training. Only the strong are allowed to fight. If they don't survive the training, they don't live, and they don't gain the honor of dying on the battle field."

Sadie sighed. "I was referring to the mess, but that information was very useful. I wish I had known."

She stood and demanded that they cease. When they didn't respond, Sadie hurled a fireball into the center of the room. That drew their attention.

"Killing yourselves to demonstrate your skills and abilities is ridiculous. You are no good to me dead. I've seen enough. You may return to your quarters and await my final decision."

Each of them bowed. Sadie bowed her head in return and watched as they left the room.

Kaiser approached Sadie with a grim look on his face. He shook his head. "I should've explained them to you. I just didn't have the chance to. You had been so busy, and—"

Sadie held up her hand. "I'm sorry. Please see to it that they are cared for and compensated for their time here."

Kaiser nodded and turned to do her bidding.

She turned to Hobson. "I have a feeling we'll have to wait on the cleanup for afterward."

"Most likely." He held his head a little straighter. "Will there be anything else?"

She thought about telling him no, but then he had

given her useful information regarding the gorgons and their penance for fighting. He could be helpful for the next demonstrations. Finally, she nodded and said, "I need you to stand by me for the demonstrations. Help me avoid another incident like that." She pointed to the blood-stained floor.

He lowered his head once. "Very well."

Sadie beckoned for the door to open with a gesture of her hand. When it responded, Mordecai entered. As he took a spot to stand in front of Sadie, a seemingly endless line of men filed into the room and stood in rows.

She leveled her gaze on Mordecai. He winked. She lifted an eyebrow and forced back the smile that tugged on her lips.

"Sadie, queen of demons, I present to you my allies, the warlocks who have no masters but pledge their loyalties to me."

She wanted to gape. Nearly fifty men stood in her throne room. They all just seemed human, but then she knew very well what they could do, having had her own battle with a warlock. But she didn't know if they would turn on her.

"Care for a demonstration, Captain?" he asked with that debonair smile of his.

"Are their skills any different from the one on topside?" she asked.

He shook his head. "Not really, just the level of

skill, power of the skill, and use varies from warlock to warlock."

"Uh, huh." She settled in her seat a bit more then asked, "I don't suppose they are demanding a demonstration of my power too, are they?"

He shook his head. "I'll cut off their heads if they dare ask."

"Very well," she said. "You may return to the barracks. I'll call for you once I have need to."

They all shook their heads, bowed after Mordecai, and followed him out of the room. She shifted her gaze to Hobson who looked at her from the corner of his eyes and seemed extremely displeased with the idea of warlocks filling the barracks of her fortress after his warnings.

"You don't need to say anything. I know what I'm doing," she said.

His words came out in a sigh. "I certainly hope you do."

Next was Damien and his witch allies. There were over thirty of them. Sadie was curious how they came to be his allies if they hadn't slept with him.

She decided to ask. "Damien, these are witches that are allied with you?"

Damien nodded. There was a glint in his eye that made Sadie narrow her eyes on him. "Care to explain that to me?"

"I haven't had sex with any of them. Instead, they

pledged themselves with blood oaths. It's not the strongest bond, as sex would make the bond unbreakable, but the blood oaths work just as well in this case. The difference is they can keep their souls. However, the bond is easily broken, so it takes some... creative methods to keep them in line and loyal to me."

Sadie lifted an eyebrow at that last part. "Why not just have sex with them and have an unbreakable bond?"

"Sex without meaning is pointless, Sadie."

She accepted that. And appreciated his honesty. "Are they part of Astrid's coven?"

"There are a handful of Astrid's coven here. They are not loyal to me, but have pledged an oath to serve in your efforts."

Sadie nodded. "Thank you. That is all. I have no need for a demonstration. Any questions?" She had addressed the group as a whole.

The murmurs became unintelligible, but one phrase stuck out above the rest. They wanted to see the amulet as proof she was indeed the demon queen.

She rolled her eyes, stood from the throne, and revealed the amulet. She even pushed into it some magic to make it glow. After a few moments, she retook her seat and asked, "Anything else?"

More murmurs, but more excited ones as they exchanged random comments between each other. Finally, some heads shook, and Damien sighed.

"I'll take that as a 'no.' Please consider yourselves at home."

Damien nodded and led the group of witches out of the room.

The next group was called forth, led by Steele as he walked in with a wink and a smile. Sadie laughed under her breath as he stopped in front of her as well.

"Let me guess," she said. "These are your succubi."

He nodded and looked over his shoulder at them. "They are."

Sadie noted there were only sixteen succubi in total, with another one seemingly royalty as she wore a circlet on her head and golden clothing that barely covered her unmentionables. She held her nose in the air, and when she looked at Sadie, her eyes narrowed.

"Can you demonstrate your powers to me?" Sadie asked.

The queen of succubi lifted an eyebrow. "I am Deseree, queen of the succubi. I shall be addressed accordingly." Her words came out sharp with a hint at something Sadie couldn't place, but she wasn't sure she wanted to either.

"Of course, Your Highness. As long as you regard me in the same respect." Sadie held her head higher and sat a bit straighter. This queen wasn't messing around. Deseree could just fuck off if she demanded respect that she wasn't willing to give in return.

The succubi queen shifted her gaze to Steele who

stood at the foot of Sadie's throne with his arms crossed over his chest. She nodded, though her fists were clenched at her sides. The other succubi behind her either shot dagger-filled glares at Sadie or looked longingly at Steele.

"What can you do?" Sadie asked.

Deseree held her head a bit higher. "We have specific skill sets that allow us to lure men and demons to their deaths. We survive on their life force and are granted powers in return for a short amount of time. Having us on your side would enable you to create distractions by separating the weaker-willed minds from the collective."

"I see," Sadie said. "I presume Steele has discussed a different form of payment to you for your services?"

"Indeed. But what we desire is our previous bargain to be upheld." The queen shifted her gaze between Sadie and Steele.

"That's not going to happen," Sadie said. "He belongs to me now and the payment we offer was more than compensating for the change in your previous agreement."

Deseree smiled. "Of course. There will always be room for further bargaining."

Sadie wasn't sure she liked the sound of that and wasn't willing to put more thought into it. It was clear she implied that they were going to get Steele one way or another.

Good luck with that.

Not.

After she proved herself as the queen of demons, the succubi seemed more willing to accept the terms of her bargain. Though, she was convinced they were still ultimately aiming for sex with Steele. She wasn't okay with that. And they needed to deal with it.

The queen had also made some veiled threats of getting Steele back while winking at him and glaring at her.

She wasn't sure she would allow them to stay in the end, but she still needed allies and an army to build against Zagan. While she wanted to give them the benefit of the doubt, something just didn't sit right with her.

Eventually, she dismissed the succubi and made her way to her room. She was tired, needed a bath, and some very much well-deserved relaxing time.

STEELE

Slipping away from his allies, he paced the hallway as something nagged at the back of his mind. The way the succubi glared at Sadie caused his blood to boil. But he knew with the current situation, they couldn't afford to dismiss anyone or lose any allies. The upcoming war with his father would be a challenge using the group they had just accumulated. Losing the succubi would make Zagan nearly unstoppable.

But he had to let them know that their behavior wouldn't be tolerated. He had to be careful of his delivery.

He considered returning to their door several times, even stopping long enough to raise his fist to knock on the door. But he never followed through. He knew the tensions were high with the new bargain of riches in place of the power they gained from having sex with him. Not to mention the best they ever had. Still, it would take a great deal of finesse and charm to make them see his reasoning. He didn't want to lose them completely, but he wouldn't tolerate disrespectful behavior toward Sadie either.

He continued pacing as he considered finding a better way to handle the situation as he couldn't rely on his knee-jerk reactions.

Eventually, he decided to give things more time to settle and adjust. When the time was right, he would handle the issue.

For now, he went to check on the barrier. This many people in the fortress made things seem more crowded, and as restless as he was, he needed some time alone to think.

SADIE

When she stepped through her door and into her room, she found Kaiser on the balcony. He faced her and smiled.

Sadie forced back a groan and said, "Not now, Kaiser. I'm too tired and I need to rest and think."

"You can do that with me right here," he said.

"I meant, I need alone time." She opened the door to her room and gestured for him to leave.

He shook his head. "You won't even know I'm here."

"Yes, I will."

"I'm not leaving," he said, firm.

"Get out!" she yelled.

"No," he said as calm as ever and planted himself against a wall.

"I have to think. I need to process my meeting with the allies, start coming up with a plan. I haven't even talked to Astrid about the damned weapon, I need sleep and peace. I need you to leave!"

"The allies are exactly the reason why I am here. I'm not willing to let you out of my sight until I know the others can be trusted."

She knew damn well that was just an excuse to stay with her. Something, however, did provoke his protective nature, and she knew there was no arguing with him once his foot was down. She sighed. "Fine."

He swooped her up with a smile and planted kisses all over her face, which caused her to giggle and kiss him back.

"Allow me to help you relax," he said and carried her to the bed.

He then laid on top of her and kissed her deeply.

Though she wouldn't let him have his way with her, she loved spending the evening making out with a side of naughty touching.

In the morning, she pulled herself away from him and dressed so she could meet with Astrid. Before leaving the room, she watched Kaiser sleep.

Damn. He was something else. She loved him. Felt even closer to him, but she really wished her men would follow her simple orders and grant her peace for once.

Shaking her head, she left her room, closing the door behind her softly.

CHAPTER TWENTY-EIGHT

SADIE

*S*adie had finally set off to meet Astrid in the war room to discuss the weapon and where it was located. It had been a long day already, and she felt like time was running out.

As she entered the room, she was shocked to find Astrid already there, staring at the maps and weapons that adorned the walls. Her arms were crossed over her chest as she looked over at Sadie when she entered the room.

"There you are. I was beginning to wonder if you were even coming," she said.

Sadie sighed. "I regret my delay in showing up here. I woke up later than expected, apparently. Thank you for waiting."

Astrid nodded. "So, what did you need to discuss? I'm assuming we're in this room for a purpose."

She nodded. "Yes. I wanted to discuss the weapon and where it is located. Can you explain what makes it so special and how it works?"

Astrid stared off, seeming to weigh the pros and cons of telling her any details. Sadie realized she may not trust her just yet. That made her slightly frustrated after what she had done to make sure the witch didn't fall into Zagan's hands. Still, she could understand her position.

"If it would help, just give me the basics," she said.

That seemed to encourage Astrid as she nodded and said, "It was created by a group of witches loyal to the previous queen. They developed and built it with special magical properties with the purpose of giving Hecate ultimate power and control over the under-world. Make her the supreme ruler."

"Thus, your hesitation to tell me about it," Sadie said. "You believe I'm walking the same path as her, don't you?"

Astrid shrugged. She narrowed her dark blue eyes on Sadie and said, "No offense, but I have every reason to be a little shy on the trust department when it comes to demons and anyone who associates with them."

"You associate yourself with Damien," Sadie added.

"Barely." She took a seat at the table. Sadie joined her.

"What else can you tell me about the weapon?"

"It is made with a variety of woods with specific magical powers from all over the world. The blade is made from the rarest steel from here in the underworld. The poison was an added little treat that was honed by one of the most powerful dark witches. It slowly eats away at the soul, rather than the flesh, when stabbed with the blade. It also has special enchantments to protect whoever wields it."

"And that's another reason you are hesitant? How powerful it could be in the wrong hands?" Sadie asked.

Astrid nodded. "That, and it was set up not to work."

Sadie leveled her gaze on the witch. Her voice came out flat when she said, "What?"

"According to legend," Astrid said, "the staff didn't work in the way it was meant to, or rather, the way Hecate wanted it to. My suspicion is that it didn't work because some of the witches were also working closely with the angels, who needed a way to ensure it was flawed."

"Of course, that makes sense."

Astrid cocked her head to the side, an expression of confusion pulled her eyebrows closer together. "It does?"

Sadie hadn't realized she said that out loud. But she decided to use the opportunity to build a little more of that trust with her. "Angels are watching out for me too. They think I'm going to turn out the same as Hecate."

"Can you really blame them?" Astrid asked.

Sadie shrugged. "I can and can't at the same time. It's complicated."

Astrid slowly nodded. "I see."

I doubt that. "I imagine Hecate, from what I have learned of her, didn't take well to the staff not working?"

Astrid let out a sarcastic laugh. "Yeah, you could say that. In a fit of rage, she locked it away and told only one witch where it was located. Before she had a chance to tell anyone, that witch disappeared. However, she was able to write the location in a book, in code. Only someone who knew the witch or knew what to look for would know what the passage meant."

"And that was the book we just risked our lives to get?" Sadie asked.

Astrid smiled and said, "Yes. Thank you again."

"It was my pleasure. Win-win, right? You get an ancient tome of your people and I get a way to defeat Zagan."

"Exactly." She smiled again, and this one was genuine, reaching her eyes and creating an almost ethereal glow around her.

"So," Sadie said, "do you think the weapon will work to knock Zagan back a few notches at least?"

"Oh yes. It is powerful, despite it not working to the degree Hecate wanted. It will definitely kill him as there is no antidote to the poison that I know of. But since I specialize in the healing arts, I could make an attempt to find one."

"No," Sadie said. "That won't be necessary. I don't want the formula to fall into Zagan's knowledge and undo everything we are trying to accomplish before we even get started."

Astrid nodded.

Sadie did the same and clutched her stomach as it growled. "Sorry. If you'll excuse me, I need to get something to eat."

"Of course," she said.

Sadie made her way toward the door. She stopped half way there and turned and faced Astrid. "Is your room okay? You're comfortable, right?"

"Yes," she said. "Thank you."

"Absolutely," she said, smiled, and finished heading out the door.

ASTRID

*A*strid made sure she wasn't followed to her room. She shut the door and set the locks with an enchantment.

She still wasn't sure of what to think of Sadie. She had seen the nice act before, and the effects of that act blowing up in a witch's face.

No thank you.

But there was something different about the queen. Astrid couldn't tell if that difference was enough to trust her entirely. She was polite, sure. Amazingly nice for a demon queen, which was seriously odd and a hard concept for the witch to wrap her mind around.

The thing she just couldn't understand, no matter how hard she tried, was the fact that she didn't want an antidote. To not have a way out of the poison in case Zagan took control of the weapon didn't make sense.

She made her way to her notes scattered along the desk on the far side of the room, she fingered them, studying the words in search of an antidote. She needed to be prepared in case things went south. And that meant making sure she had perfected the cure for the poison before the weapon could be used.

Especially against her.

CHAPTER TWENTY-NINE

DAMIEN

*W*ith too much energy to burn off and not a hell of a lot to do, he decided to challenge his brothers to a match in the training room of the castle.

He found each of them in separate areas of the castle, but each of them just as eager to have something to do besides babysit their allies. Steele was in the hall of the west wing, not too far from the room his succubi allies were staying in. He stared at the ceiling, sitting in an armless chair with two of his legs up in the air, and his head resting on the wall.

"Don't you look as happy as a lark in a windowsill," Damien said.

Steele shifted his eyes only to look at his brother and then they rolled. "Brother, this is a moment of celebration. Can't you see I'm too busy in my thrilling excitement to talk?"

Damien chuckled. "Oh, yes." He kicked the legs of the chair that were hovering in the air and brought Steele upright in a sudden shift in movement. He glared at him, but that only caused him to laugh again. "Come on, I have an idea."

"Oh, do keep the suspense going by the oh so tempting words you just said." Steele didn't move. He crossed his arms over his chest and leaned back against the chair, crossing his legs at the ankles.

"What if I told you there was a chance to beat me in a challenge?" he added.

Steele's breath caught in his chest and he inched his gaze to Damien's, a mischievous tilt to his lips. Damien had him right where he wanted him. Putty in his hands.

Steele narrowed his eyes on his brother. "You lie."

Damien shrugged. "Guess you'll have to find out."

Without another word, Damien turned on his heels and headed down the hall to find either Kaiser or Mordecai. He knew Steele would follow. He was too much of a jokester to resist the temptation of what he had just offered. None of his brothers would.

Mordecai was just leaving the barracks where his warlocks were stationed. There was a glint in his eyes as he met Damien's. He recognized that look. It was annoyance. Which played well with Damien's plans.

"Warlocks giving you hell?" he asked.

Mordecai said, "Not now, brother." He passed his brother and continued on without missing a beat.

Damien shrugged and followed him out of the barracks. "So, I made this deal with Steele that he couldn't beat me."

Mordecai snorted. "What else is new?"

"What if I said you had to fight with him?"

Mordecai hesitated, stopping mid-step and turning his head to gaze over his shoulder. He didn't answer though.

"Come on. We haven't sparred in a while, brother."

"Last week."

Damien ignored the interruption and continued. "I promise it will be worth your while. Work out those frustrations on me."

Mordecai faced his brother. "Steele bought this?" He shook his head. "Unbelievable."

"Please." That word sounded horrible coming out of his mouth. Mordecai must have caught the same as he lifted an eyebrow in response. Damien cleared his throat and said. "Meet me in the training room. Unless you're scared that I'm going to defeat you."

Mordecai laughed. Full-bellied, loud, boisterous. "Yeah, okay. I'll be there. This is something I gotta see." He turned and continued on to whatever or wherever he was set on before Damien stopped him.

All that was left was getting Kaiser to join in on the fun.

Damien made his way to the grounds after checking the rest of the barracks for him and not finding him. As he reached the door, Kaiser entered and stared at his brother with a look of confusion.

"Just the man I was looking for," Damien said with a smile.

"Do I want to know?" Kaiser asked.

"Got a challenge for you," he said, joining his brother's side. "Are you interested?"

Kaiser shrugged. "Sure, why not."

"That was easy! Beat me to the training room." Damien took off.

He laughed as he heard Kaiser curse behind him. However, Kaiser had beaten him to the training room. Damien walked in as all three brothers looked at each other and then to him.

"Well," Mordecai said, "we're all here. Now what?"

"A wager," Damien said, voice dark and a hint of a smile toying with his lips.

"On...?" Kaiser said.

Damien held up a finger and wagged it in front of him. "First, the rules. No cheating. We face off with each other, ultimate winner gets to spend time with Sadie."

"What if the winner was already next?" Steele asked.

Damien nodded and said, "Then his time doubles."

"What if Sadie doesn't go with it?" Kaiser asked, crossing his arms in front of him with his feet shoulder-width apart.

"I think she will." Damien walked to the center of the room. "Any other questions?"

"What if the loser's time was next?" Mordecai asked.

Damien chuckled. "Then it sucks to be the loser. He'll lose the time."

The looks on his brothers' faces were priceless. They all appeared eager to get started and seemed to unconsciously flex their muscles and stretch their wings. Good. He needed this, and so did they.

"Anything else?" Damien asked, knowing he had his brothers right where he wanted them.

Mordecai nodded. "Yeah. Who's first?"

Damien pointed to him. "You and I will fight each other, and Steele and Kaiser will fight at the same time. Winners from those rounds will then fight and whoever wins that match will be the winner."

"Simple," Steele said.

Kaiser snorted.

"Ready?" Damien asked.

Each of the brothers faced their opponent and took their battle stance. Mordecai's glare was meant to shake his nerves, but instead, he winked and that set Mordecai to attack.

His brother, unsurprisingly, shifted into shadow right as Damien's fist was set to collide with his jaw. The shadow form shifted to behind Damien, and he kicked his leg back into Mordecai's gut as he shifted back into his natural form. Mordecai grunted.

"You'll have to try harder than that, brother," Damien said as he shifted his stance to face him again and prepared for another attack.

"Fair enough," he said, shifting to shadow and moving quicker.

But Damien wasn't caught off guard so easily and landed a blow to his brother's chest, again as he solidified. Mordecai leveled his gaze on him after he recovered from the hit. Damien chuckled and shrugged.

Mordecai charged him, knocking Damien to the ground, where they wrestled, landing punches to each other's sides and flipping over to try and dominate the other. Damien couldn't help laughing.

Now that's the spirit!

He even landed a good hit to Damien's jaw, which fueled his fun even more. Damien put Mordecai in a headlock to which he received a well-played elbow to the ribs.

"I thought you said no cheating?" Mordecai asked, voice dark with a hint of anger.

That only roused Damien more. "I haven't cheated. I'm just better than you, brother."

"Oh yeah?" Mordecai shifted to shadow again and

solidified a few feet from Damien. He had summoned his staff and held it aimed at Damien's head.

Damien climbed to his feet and stood tall, nose angled in the air. "Your move."

"Checkmate. Submit." Mordecai jabbed his staff at the air between them.

He chuckled and said, "Never." And charged.

Mordecai swung his staff toward the back of Damien's knees, which he knew was coming. He had counted on him to try and disarm him by knocking him to the floor. He stretched out an arm at the last second before hitting the ground and hooked Mordecai's knee, pulling him down as well.

They landed with a thump, the air being knocked from the both of them. Damien laughed again. "You still haven't beaten me, yet!"

"Oh, don't you worry," Mordecai said as he landed a knee to Damien's gut. "I've only just begun."

As they wrestled, Damien thought about this being exactly what he needed.

CHAPTER THIRTY

STEELE

*A*s Damien and Mordecai sparred, Steele faced off with Kaiser. It was an incredibly fun fight considering Kaiser had a hard time working through Steele's illusion.

He had made it so Sadie was the one he fought. It was endearing and somewhat pathetic how quickly Kaiser's eyes softened at the image. Steele pranced around Kaiser, slowly circling him and watching the amusing display.

That was until Kaiser flipped around and nailed a punch to Steele's cheek. That knocked him back a few steps and the illusion faltered. Damn, he'd have to be prepared for that in the heat of battle. Illusions could be very powerful and useful, but one unlucky swing of a fist or weapon could cause trouble for him.

Steele rubbed his cheek and smiled. "Not bad,

brother. I didn't think you would be able to break away from that one."

"It's a low blow, even for you, to use Sadie as a weapon." Kaiser kicked toward Steele's gut, but he quickly blocked the blow and landed a punch to his brother's chest.

"Come now, we all love Sadie... just some of us are weaker than others," Steele said and dodged the blow that would've landed on his nose. He laughed.

"What's the matter Steele? Can't fight without cheating?" Kaiser teased.

Steele stopped laughing and stood still, serious as ever then, cast an illusion that created six of himself while he charged at Kaiser.

"There's the challenge I was looking for," he said as he dodged blows from all the fake Steeles.

One landed in his gut, and he gripped Steele's wrist and twisted, rolling out of the way so that he stood behind him, still holding onto the hand.

"Not bad brother," Steele said, gritting against the sharp stabbing sensation shooting through his wrist. "But not good enough."

Steele bowed forward, taking Kaiser along, flipping him onto his back on the floor then quickly climbed on top of him, pinning his hands to the floor and making noises from his throat to get a ball of spit to drip onto his brother's face.

Kaiser said, "You wouldn't dare."

Steele gulped and smiled. "Well, now I have to start over."

Kaiser bucked Steele off of him. Steele rolled to his feet and stood, ready for the next bout of action his brother was bound to deliver him.

Steele loved this game. He needed to thank Damien when he got the chance. It was a nice break from the tension of planning, war, fight, and planning some more. Plus, it gave him a sense of closeness he had missed from his years of estrangement from his brothers. Ever since Zagan killed their brother, Cedric, they had been at war with each other. Distrusting of their own blood. Part of him had wondered if his brothers truly hated him. Or if they still wished he had been in Cedric's place. But when Sadie came into their lives, things changed—he changed.

His brothers weren't his enemies. Either way, it was their father who drove the wedge between him and his siblings. Soon, that threat will be gone, and they could be a family again.

They moved well together. And they fought well together. Even against one another. Somehow, Steele even knew that they worked best together, fighting side by side as opposed to fighting individually.

His father may have believed them weak and unworthy to succeed his throne, but the four of them were a formidable force when together. Perhaps Zagan actually feared that truth. Well, he wasn't going to let their father or anyone else get in their way or separate them, especially now that they had Sadie to protect. And they'd do it as a family.

He missed his brothers, though he would never admit to it out loud. And this was exactly what he needed. Time with them.

CHAPTER THIRTY-ONE

SADIE

*S*adie decided training would do her some good. Help her work out the kinks in the current plan. However, when she walked into the training room, she stopped mid-step and stared at her men practicing coordinated training and moves.

As she watched, she noticed how each of them complemented the others in terms of strength and power. They worked well together as a team.

Some of the sigils on Mordecai's body glowed and shifted. His hands turned to shadow, extending a dark, shadowy substance as a barrier between them and the practice target. That allowed Kaiser to zoom through, under the cover of his brother's shadowy darkness, and hit the target with a blast of fire.

Hmm... Sadie considered that a deadly combination against any foe on the battlefield. She was impressed with that move.

Damien wielded his sword blindfolded. Steele had the look of concentration on his face and she wondered if he was using his telepathic abilities to guide his brother in striking down opponents. He moved well. And he managed to disarm each target set up around him. The constant coordination with his brother would make it easy for him in the midst of a crowd to take down any target.

In this moment, she realized she made the absolute best decision in choosing all four of them. That decision gifted her the four most powerful warriors to fight beside her. And that made her feel even stronger and more capable to handle anything that came her way.

After waiting a few minutes to see if any of them would realize she was there, watching them, and none of them having done so, she cleared her throat.

The men stopped what they were doing to face her. Each of them smiled.

"Having fun?" she asked, faking pointed expressions at them and standing with her arms crossed over her chest, though her cheeks fought against her on hiding the smile that pulled at the corners of her lips.

They separated from one another and stood a bit straighter, fixing their clothes and hair as they stood.

Damien said, "We were just spending a little time playing around. That's all."

Steele shook his head. "Essentially, yes. We were having fun."

"So, who won the bet?" Mordecai asked.

"What bet?" Sadie asked as she narrowed her eyes on the men. When they told her, she groaned and rolled her eyes. "Stop using me as your reward! I'm not a toy or a prize. Sheesh."

"What brings you to grace us with your presence?" Kaiser asked.

Sadie sighed. "I spoke with Astrid about the weapon. And it looks like it will likely be guarded, just like everything else we have tried to get."

Damien said, "Fret not, my dear. We have ways of being able to get through creatures. If Astrid can't tame 'em, we certainly will."

"Yeah," Mordecai said, "But having the former would help Sadie with her forces."

She nodded. "That's very true. However, we shouldn't assume Astrid would be willing to do so. She should be asked first. Though, I would love to see her in action some more. This would be a great opportunity."

The men agreed, and she felt relieved. Now on to the next item on the agenda.

"That's not all. We need to take care of the garden and Hecate. With the allies here, I don't want them prancing off and stumbling across her. She's stayed beyond her welcome. Something needs to be done."

Kaiser stepped forward. "Not that I don't agree with something needing to be done with the ghost. I have to say that I'm not okay with you going in there again. At all. You nearly died the last time. There's a very real possibility you won't make it out again."

She nodded. "True. But I have to put my foot down. Ghost or no. She's in my home and will not threaten me."

"What's the plan, Captain?" Mordecai asked.

"First, you need to shower. Let's run a check on the barrier and get some supplies gathered. We'll need to plan how to get the staff and set a date for that. Once we have the staff, we'll figure out a way to deal with Hecate."

The men agreed, and they set off. Sadie stared at the empty room and wondered about the way her men moved together as a unit. She didn't want to see harm come to them and wondered if there was a way to make sure they would be safe during the upcoming battle.

She considered a war plan. One they all could agree on. But for now, the barrier needed tending to. The wards needed checked, and she needed to make sure they first set a plan for the staff.

CHAPTER THIRTY-TWO

STEELE

*H*aving had that impromptu sparring session with his brothers, Steele felt more level-headed to face the succubi without pushing them away and losing them as allies completely. He strode down the hall to their door and knocked. No one answered.

Frowning, he opened the door and found that they were all in a circle, on their knees, crying. The lights were dimmed, and the shadows seemed to move with a life of their own. That unsettled him as he knew there were very few reasons for succubi to cry. One was to lure men to their deaths by catering to their natural need to rescue damsels in distress, not to mention their need to protect. And reason number two was when a death occurred.

With the recent change in their bargaining, Steele

was leaning more toward the first rather than the second. Besides, this fortress was safe for everyone. No one could have possibly died.

"Nice try, ladies. Crocodile tears don't work on me."

Deseree stood, turned, and faced Steele, sniffing and wiping her eyes with the tips of her fingers. "This isn't some ploy to get you in bed, you idiot. Kinna is dead."

His eyebrows knitted together. "Who?"

She leveled her gaze on him, eyes turning red. "Kinna. My best servant and adopted daughter. She was who I chose to succeed me."

Steele shook his head then wove his way through the weeping collection of women to the mound at the center of them covered by silks and jewels.

"What happened?" he asked, unable to hide the anger in his voice.

"Isn't it obvious?" the queen asked. "Your queen killed her."

Oh shit. This isn't good. Steele had to defuse the situation and fast. There was no way Sadie did this. He had to make her see that too. "Deseree, what makes you think Sadie killed your servant?"

"She's jealous of what we had. She is trying to keep you under her thumb and control you. Can't you see that?"

He sighed and placed his hands on the tops of her

arms. "Please, try to understand she isn't like Hecate. She's different. And I know that's hard to accept with the history."

"She's enchanted you, Steele. You're too under her spell to realize what she's doing to you. Look at what she did to Kinna!"

"How do you know Sadie is responsible?" he asked, trying to maintain his patience during her time of need but really getting annoyed that she was convinced Sadie had ulterior motives.

Deseree pressed her lips tightly together and went to the body and pulled on the sheet that covered her favorite servant. Deep gouging claw marks slashed open her neck and some on her torso. The poor girl's eyes were fixed on fear.

"She never came back after we sent her for wine. Another one of my servants found her." She sniffed as weeping continued even louder.

"Sadie didn't cause this. But I promise, I will get to the bottom of this."

"It has to be. Who else could have done such a horrible thing?" Deseree asked, falling into sobs once more.

Steele tried to think of any of the other allies in the fortress that would have the ability to create such wounds and came up short. He shook his head. "I will find out. As soon as I know, you will be the first I tell. Meanwhile, prepare her for her journey. As payment for your services in the coming war and for the trouble of losing your best servant, I will bring you fine silks and even rarer and finer gems than those previously promised."

"What about an uptick in power. It will help us in the battle."

Of course, they would still push for sex with him. "No," he said. "I highly suggest you follow my original instructions and stay in this room. I'll see to it that you are provided drink and food."

"I'm afraid you will have to do better than gems and fabric. If you cannot promise us that and our safety by giving us what we need to protect ourselves, then we have no choice but to return to our own home." Deseree kept her words even, and never shifted her gaze from his eyes.

She was serious.

Despite his efforts otherwise, it seemed they would lose his allies after all. He still needed to find out what happened to the girl and why. And he would. Regardless if they stayed or not. If someone was sneaking around killing off allies, that meant Sadie could be in danger as well. And that was not something he was willing to bargain for.

He turned on his heels without another word and left.

CHAPTER THIRTY-THREE

*A*s soon as Sadie walked through the front door of her fortress, Steele had glued himself to her side. Though it seemed odd for him to constantly be near her, rather, practically on top of her, she didn't think much of it. Kaiser was equally as attached at the hip for a bit after she returned from her trip to pick up Astrid. It seemed like his way of getting a little more time with her. So, she dealt with it.

She summoned Hobson, as she allowed Steele to hold and kiss her. Within moments, ever dependable, the gargoyle showed up and cleared his throat. She pulled from him and smiled at her butler.

"You summoned me?" he asked.

"Yes. I need all possible locations the queen would

hide stuff she didn't want anyone to have. Can you get me a list?"

He shook his head. "Sadly, I wasn't privileged to that sort of information. My apologies, but I cannot help with this one."

She waved her hand through the air. "Don't worry about it, Hobson. We'll figure it out. Thank you anyway."

The succubi entered the foyer of the fortress and Steele visibly stiffened, standing even closer to Sadie. She rolled her eyes and took a step back. She did value personal space, and she could only handle him being on top of her for so long. Besides, now wasn't the time to be needy. The succubi were obviously needing something and she needed to put her crown on and play queen for a moment.

Deseree, the queen, wouldn't look at Sadie. Instead, she addressed Steele, and him alone. "We are leaving now."

"Well that's unfortunate. Why, pray-tell, are you leaving?" Sadie asked.

The succubus queen shifted her ruthless gaze to her and narrowed her eyes. "You should already know. After all, it's by your doing."

Sadie clenched her jaw and her hands balled into fists at her sides. "I beg your pardon?" It was more of a statement than a question, and she let her anger slip into her words.

Steele stepped between the two of them. "There's been an attack. A servant was killed, and she happened to have been Deseree's favorite servant. She believes you had something to do with the murder." He added in the description of the gashes which puzzled Sadie. She didn't know of any one in her fortress that would have the capability to cause such injuries, much less herself.

As though to further prove Steele's words, the group separated to show a body covered in silk and jewels carried on a makeshift gurney.

"I assure you," she said to the succubus queen, "that I had nothing to do with any deaths under this roof." She shifted to Hobson. "Has anyone entered the fortress unannounced? I haven't sensed anything."

Hobson closed his eyes and took a deep breath. When he opened them, he shook his head and said, "No. I don't sense anything unusual either. No one who shouldn't be in the fortress has been within so much as the gate. The defenses would have stripped the intruder bare."

"As I thought," she said and turned to the succubus queen. "I'll make sure we find answers to the death of your servant and will deal with the perpetrator accordingly."

She rolled her eyes and shook her head. "Your word is not good enough. I want sex with Steele." Her eyes hungrily ran over Steele's body.

Sadie scoffed. "Well, that's out of the question. The previous forms of payment and the promise of due course with the murder is all I can do."

Deseree turned without another word and headed through a portal. Her servants followed, as their sullen faces were streaked with tears. They carried the body through as well, and once the last succubus was through, the portal sealed, leaving Sadie, Hobson, and Steele in thick silence.

Steele shuffled beside her and huffed. "I'm sorry for the loss of my allies."

Sadie leveled her gaze on him then took his face into her hands, making sure he couldn't look away. "Don't be. I don't blame you. Though the drop in numbers is a cause for concern, we will make do with who we have now. Perhaps the succubi will have a change of heart before the battle starts."

Astrid entered the room, slowing down as though entering a cloud of tension that filled the air just moments before the succubi queen arrived. The negative energy still hadn't managed to fully clear out.

"I hope I'm not interrupting anything," she said.

Sadie gestured for her to approach. "Of course not."

Smiling, she held up a small stone that reminded Sadie of river rock between her finger and thumb. Except, this one was iridescent and blue. "This is a charm I created in hopes that it would help us hone in on the location of the staff. I took the liberty of testing it out on a local map from your war room. It works, and I think we have a general location to hunt."

"Excellent, where?" Sadie asked. Astrid was certainly proving herself more and more a valuable part of the team.

Her eyebrows knitted themselves together. "Some place called the Darkhaven Caverns. It's not far from here, and the best part is this will glow brighter the closer we get to the staff. Pretty cool, huh?"

Sadie said, "Yes. Very much so."

"Great. When do we set off?" she asked.

Sadie thought for a moment. There was no telling when Zagan would return. He was likely amassing an even larger army. They ran the risk of not having enough time to get the staff and return before he did show up. Now was ideal.

"How about immediately?" Sadie asked.

The men collectively agreed with either a nod or a verbal response.

Damien added, "There's one problem though."

Sadie narrowed her eyes on him and propped a hand on her hip. "What's that?"

"There are too many people here that have pledged their magic and sword to you. These are demons we are talking about as well. The fortress, more specifically the one that belongs to the demon queen, is way too much of an opportunity for mutiny." He leveled his gaze on her. "There's already been one murder. Let's not invite more."

Sadie nodded. "True. At least until we discover who is responsible for that death, we should have at least two of us stay behind. I'm going and so will Astrid. Damien, you are my second in command. You should stay here and keep everyone in line. Mordecai can help with reconnaissance."

They both nodded.

"So, any ideas on how to get to this location?" Sadie asked the men.

Steele nodded as he rubbed his chin. "I suppose we could even portal there, but I haven't personally been there."

"I have," Kaiser said. "It would be tricky still. The terrain is unsteady in much of the area. I suggest a portal just outside the entrance."

Mordecai huffed. "Has anyone noticed that each location we've had to go to so far has had some level of peril? You should walk the whole way."

"That would take too much time, I would think," Sadie said. "A portal would be quicker. And with Kaiser having been there, he could land us in a safe spot. That would save us a lot of time. Besides, the sooner we can get the staff, the sooner we can return and be that much more ready to face Zagan."

Mordecai mumbled something under his breath, drawing Sadie's attention. She smiled at him and said,

"I appreciate your concern for us. Have faith in your brothers and me. We'll be back before you know it."

"If we are going to leave here soon," Astrid said, "I need a moment to gather some supplies and things I may need for the trip. I want to be prepared for anything."

Sadie faced Astrid and nodded. "Very well. I suggest we all do the same and meet back here. Meanwhile, Damien and Mordecai," she faced the both of them, "see what you can find out about the murder. We'll need to figure out if anyone else in the fortress is in danger and seclude the perpetrator immediately. I suggest the dungeon with extra wards."

They both nodded and took turns wrapping her in their arms and giving her a long kiss goodbye.

Once they were out of sight, she turned to Hobson. "Make sure you keep an eye out for them. I don't want anything to happen while I'm gone."

"I'll spare both eyes as often as I can, Your Majesty." He nodded and headed down one of the halls that led off from the foyer.

"All right, let's get this over with," she said to Astrid, Kaiser, and Steele. Each of them nodded and headed their separate ways to get ready. Sadie made her way to her room for more practical gear and clothing.

CHAPTER THIRTY-FOUR

SADIE

While waiting for Astrid to gather a few last-minute things she needed, Sadie practiced with her shadow sword. Whatever the witch expected, she apparently wanted to be overprepared. Sadie could appreciate that, although she hoped it wasn't so much overpreparation that she would end up slowing them down.

A loud, ear-splitting scream echoed down the halls and toward Sadie. It was a chilling, blood-curdling sound that caused goosebumps to rise on her arms. Whoever made that sound was in deep trouble.

Sadie jumped into action. She ran, sword in hand, toward the direction of the sound. On the way, her men joined her. Even Astrid rushed into the hall as they made their way to whoever was in trouble.

"What was that sound?" Astrid asked.

"We're about to find out," Sadie said as she turned and stopped mid-run. Her men joined her at her side as she stared into the shadow filled hall where a figure leaned over a body lying limp on the floor.

Cautiously, Sadie moved forward, not wanting to scare off the figure and lose their only chance at catching the murderer within her own home. As she drew closer, she recognized the woman as one of Damien's witch allies. The poor girl had the same gashes that matched the succubus's from Steele's descriptions earlier.

The figure hovering over the witch stood straighter, and Sadie instantly knew who she was.

Hecate. The fucking bitch.

She was in nearly full physical form, sucking the life out of the witch.

Hecate twisted and set her eyes on Sadie. She glared. "You!" It came out in a growl. "You stole my pendant and my fortress. You have no right to my kingdom. I will soon be strong enough to get you, Sadie, and when that day comes, I'll take back what you have stolen."

Okay, time to handle this.

Sadie's blood boiled, and she stood her ground as she bit back every last ounce of self-control. "I'm the thief? I didn't ask for this. It was given to me. You're dead! You left your fortress and meandered the south wing like a coward! Now you are preying on my allies like you have a right to their life. Huh-uh. Wrong choice. We end this. And we end this now!"

Hecate laughed, dark and sinister as she sauntered slowly toward Sadie. "Is that what you wish, little human? Oh, this is going to be so much fun."

The space between them disappeared as the previous demon queen swooped in closer and slashed out a taloned hand at Sadie's chest.

"I'm going to take back what you stole from me!" she said, seething the words between clenched teeth.

Sadie tried to fight off the previous queen as her men worked to keep her busy by pulling her attention from Sadie and to them. She used their cover to launch a few fireballs at Hecate. She also used her sword and managed to get in a few shallow cuts before Hecate deflected the blade, making it nearly impossible for her to be killed.

Even Steele's illusions weren't able to distract the woman for long.

This wasn't good. Not only was the previous queen gaining more of a physical form each time they had an encounter with her, she was also gaining her strength back. Which was the last thing Sadie needed at the moment.

She heard Astrid uttering an incantation. She looked over her shoulder and said, "Stay back!"

Astrid nodded and took a few steps back and ducked into the bend of the hallway.

Sadie returned her attention to the previous queen who had just attempted to slash Damien's throat with her claws.

Oh no she just did not.

Sadie's amulet warmed. Energy pooled through her arms and pulsed at her hands, accumulating in strength and power.

"Back off, bitch!" she said and held her hands toward Hecate. Streams of purple-blue lighting shot from her hands. At the same time, Damien lunged with Lightbane to keep her hands busy from blocking the magic, and Mordecai shifted into shadow form, bending around the bolts of lightning to keep the previous queen's eyes from being locked on Sadie. Kaiser shot balls of fire at the queen, and Steele stood back with that concentrated expression on his face, likely an illusion that was finally working on the queen.

Once the lightning ended, the queen had fallen to her knees. Sadie conjured her shadow sword again and pointed its tip at Hecate's neck. "Leave here and *never* come back."

Hecate narrowed her eyes on Sadie. If looks could kill, she was sure that was the previous queen's intent. Lucky for her, they didn't. She summoned Hobson who appeared within moments and gripped the woman from behind, tugging her arms behind her and yanked her to her feet. She groaned against the pain and Sadie found satisfaction in that.

Just as Sadie was about to deal her death blow, her amulet's magic seeped through her skin, but it wasn't the fire she was accustomed to. It was cold. The sensation of the tips of her fingers tingled and burned as well, reminding her of times she went outside in frigid temps without gloves on. Within seconds, a flood of white light burst from her fingers. It surrounded Hecate as she screamed.

"This isn't the last you've seen of me," she said, seething. "I'll be back to reclaim what is mine."

The light expanded, swelling to an orb that fully encompassed her and a small area around her. Her men jumped back. Sadie took a step back herself. And in the blink of an eye, the orb of light burst, leaving a stark darkness in the hall for a short moment.

Once her eyes adjusted to the sudden lack of light, she looked around for any sign of the dead demon queen. There was none.

"What happened?" Sadie asked.

Hobson cleared his throat. "If I may, Your Majesty…"

"Yes, please," she said, gesturing for him to continue.

"It appears that you banished Hecate from the grounds. I felt the shift in the energy of the fortress once it was complete."

Sadie stared at her hands and thought about that nice tidbit of information. She had learned something new about her amulet's magic. It protected her once, just before she was brought here to the fortress, but it seemed to have protected her again.

"I also noticed that Hecate was preparing a counter spell for you. She would've likely killed you had she completed the spell," Hobson added, a look of concern marred his stony features. He seemed genuinely concerned with Sadie's safety. "She won't be allowed to cross the barrier if she does come back."

And she will. She had no doubts about the next time they would meet--one of them would die. But Sadie would be damned if it were her.

Hobson nodded. "But at least for now, she can't get back in and hurt anyone else within these walls." He turned toward Sadie. "That, in and of itself, is a victory."

"We'll have to keep her sneaky attacks in mind for when she does show back up. And she will. She'll want her throne back. That much has already been established."

She turned her attention toward her men, checking to make sure they were uninjured. Beyond a few close calls with the razor like talons from Hecate, they were relatively unscathed. She sighed in relief. Astrid came up and seemed a little paler than usual. With the loss of a coven sister, it didn't surprise Sadie.

Sadie said, "I'm sorry. I had no idea that—"

Astrid held up her hand and shook her head. "Don't. It's not your fault. I'm fine. We all are, and that's what's important."

She nodded, grateful they all managed to make it through that fight without more serious injuries. Hecate would need more time to regain her strength and form, which galled Sadie, but at least it would give her the time she needed to get the staff and take care of Zagan. Then she'd handle the former demon queen.

As Damien gathered up the body of his fallen ally, they decided to make their way to the foyer and discuss what to do with the witch.

Hobson met them in the hall. "It is done, Your Majesty."

"Good," Sadie said. "I hope she didn't give you too much problem."

The gargoyle shook his head. "She did not." His gaze shifted to the witch in Damien's arms. He shook his head with a frown. "I would be honored to give her a final resting place on the fortress grounds."

Damien hesitated then looked to Astrid. She nodded. Sadie did too. With a sigh, he handed over the witch's body.

"I'll go with him to prepare her body for the afterlife," Astrid said, voice soft and sad. "I'll come back with some healing salve for your wound."

Oh, right. Sadie had forgotten about her own

injuries. She had been too wrapped up in the loss and the fight with the previous queen that she hadn't thought about her own afflictions. Her chest was cut up pretty badly from the nails that wretched pseudo-ghost had used to claw out the amulet. Luckily, the bleeding had stopped, and the wounds started to seal, but the process was slow, and the salve would likely help with the speed. However, her shirt was destroyed.

So help Sadie, she'd end that bitch once and for all when the time came.

"I'm not convinced that is the last we've seen of that woman," Mordecai said. "We need to set up guards."

"Agreed," Damien said, and he and Mordecai set off to take care of that. Steele and Kaiser joined them.

Meanwhile, Sadie headed to her room to change again and wait for the salve.

*S*adie sat on a lounge, enjoying the peace and quiet of her room. She had left her shirt off and allowed a flow of fresh air to the slashes on her chest. A knock softly rapped on her door. She beckoned the door open with a hand gesture. Astrid stood on the other side with a stone container in her hand.

She smiled and said, "I have the salve."

Sadie nodded. "Good, come in."

Astrid did so and crossed the floor to Sadie. The gashes had begun to seal, but the process was slower than Sadie liked. She reclined on the lounge and allowed Astrid to put the substance over the open wounds. The smell was heavy of menthol and a slight, sweet lavender scent. As the cool gel-like substance was rubbed in, it warmed her skin.

"Thank you," Sadie said.

Astrid hesitated, and her eyebrows knitted together. "Um... you're welcome."

That's right. She was demon queen and still getting used to everyone thinking she was a badass with no manners and didn't know how to show a lick of gratitude. So be it. She hoped kindness—a rarity in this world of greed—would make the creatures of the underworld more inclined to follow her. That had helped her princes fall for her. Instead of a show of force, having people see her as a compassionate ruler seemed a better idea and fell in line with the way Sadie really was. However, she wouldn't take any crap and had showed that a number of times already.

"That should do it. It'll take a while, but you'll be good as new in no time." Astrid slapped a lid onto the container and turned to walk away.

Sadie pulled herself into a seated position and said, "I appreciate your help. If you hold on a moment, we can walk together." She grabbed her shirt—a simple t-shirt—and slipped it on.

"Sure."

Sadie stood and stretched, reaching her arms behind her. There was no tenderness or pain. "Huh. That stuff is amazing."

Astrid nodded. "It really works well for many injuries. I'm glad it's helping."

"Me too." Sadie joined Astrid at the center of her room and said, "Ready?"

"About as ready as I'll ever be," she said.

The first part of their trek was silent. But Sadie could tell Astrid was working through something that puzzled her. She had an intense look on her face and a slight wrinkle formed just above the bridge of her nose. Sadie wanted to ask about that but decided that she would let Astrid speak when she was ready to.

And she did.

"You're not what I expected," she finally said.

Sadie laughed. "I get that a lot."

"I bet."

"I wasn't sure what to expect when meeting you," Sadie said. "I had never, to my knowledge, met a witch before. And Damien and Mordecai showed me the darker ones before we made it to you, so it was something of a relief to see how down to earth and real you are."

"Real?" she laughed. "As opposed to fake?"

Sadie joined in on the laughter. "No, down to earth, relaxed, genuine. You know, that kind of stuff."

Astrid nodded. "I guess we are alike in the sense we still maintain our human decency."

"Yes," Sadie said with a big smile. "Very much so."

They rounded the corner of the hall that led into the foyer. Kaiser and Steele looked to them expectantly, like they had been waiting an obscene amount of time for them to finally show up.

Steele approached with a mischievous grin. "Are we ready, ladies?"

"I think so," Astrid said. "But I'm not sure if we are talking about the same thing."

"Trust me," Sadie said. "We're not." She pointed a finger at Steele, "And that's never gonna happen."

"We'll see," he said and glided toward the door.

Sadie shook her head. Always the jokester. But she loved that about him. He made her relax more when things got a bit too serious. She appreciated that.

Kaiser opened the door and they all step outside. Just before they reached the gates, a sensation of warning, of someone having crossed her barrier, came over her. She and Kaiser exchanged knowing looks and prepared for a fight.

Once they neared the gates, deep within the shadows of the woods were a group of demons and witches. They stepped forward, seething and glaring between Sadie and Astrid.

"Zagan has a message for the one who claims herself queen, and for the witch that hides in her shadow." A witch, mean looking, ugly, and possibly decaying a little, judging by the rotting flesh on her cheek, had spoken and pointed a finger at Sadie.

She arched an eyebrow and crossed her arms over her chest. "Oh, is that so? Is he quitting? Got his butt kicked and now he's got his tail tucked between his legs, busying himself with licking his wounds?"

The group scoffed.

The witch said, "Funny. We have a clever one, boys." She laughed and twisted to look at her backup who also chuckled with her. "Reconsider, or submit to the wrath he will bring upon you."

"And what?" Sadie said. "I suppose you're that wrath?"

Though she knew Zagan's tactics were sometimes hard to follow, there was definitely something more to this visit. Sadie just couldn't figure out what yet.

"Wanna find out?" the witch asked, her hands took on a green, smoky glow.

"Maybe. But here's the thing—Zagan will never get my alliance. Come fire, brimstone, or anything else that he throws at us, I will never bow down to him. Got it? Now, before you die, you should consider returning to him with my response."

"I was hoping you would say that," the witch said. "Get 'em!"

The group charged.

Kaiser stepped in front of Sadie and blocked the first demon that attempted to strike Sadie with his sword. It had a purplish-black aura and she wondered what power it had, how bad it would've hurt.

But that lasted a split-second as she summoned her shadow sword and went after the next demon that tried to disarm Kaiser while he fought the first one. She landed a killing blow on the first try then went for the witch who tried to conjure thick vines with bleeding thorns to capture Sadie.

She slashed at them as they grew and closed the space between the two of them. The witch smirked. Sadie had a few choice words on the tip of her tongue, but the glint in the witch's eyes put her on high alert. She dodged the attack of vines that came up from behind her. She rolled behind the witch and impaled her with the sword in her back.

The vines withered into ashes.

When Sadie stood, she saw Astrid, Steele, and Kaiser had the other demons surrounded and clustered together. One of them screamed in agony.

Sadie smiled. *That's my Steele.*

Kaiser set fire to another, and Astrid simply held her hands in front of her as bolts of electricity danced between her splayed out fingers. She had a devious smile tugging on her lips and sent out pulses of electricity to zap the other demon who didn't seem to see that coming.

Sadie realized Steele had each demon under a different illusion.

The screaming demon collapsed on the ground dead, leaving his comrades alone. Steele broke his illusion and asked, "Shall I continue with more fun ways of torture, or have you had enough?"

The demons stuttered and sputtered out incoherent words as they took steps backward to get away from the three. Astrid sent another zap to one of the demons and they stumbled over themselves, falling to the ground, and scrambling to get back to their feet.

They took off running in the direction they came from as one promised they would return.

"We'll get our revenge on the battle field," he promised.

Sadie watched them run away like the cowards they were. Fat chance.

As the others joined Sadie, she exchanged glances with each of them, and they simultaneously busted out in laughter.

Between bouts of laughter and gasps for air, Sadie asked, "Think you could portal us from here?"

Kaiser nodded and wiped his eyes. He took a few calming breaths and focused himself. A ball of light formed, and the portal widened to allow all of them through. Joining hands, they jumped through. The sensation of falling made the pit of Sadie's stomach clench.

That was always the worst part of portals.

CHAPTER THIRTY-SIX

SADIE

*A*s soon as they landed, the ground shook violently beneath their feet. Kaiser and Steele instinctively covered Sadie and Astrid until the vibrations stopped. Once they did, Sadie stood straight and looked around them. The ceiling was rotted away like holes had eaten into the stone, and many larger pieces had collapsed to the ground. Rocks tremored and fell around them ever so often.

The life around them seemed faded and dulled. This place was dying. No wonder Kaiser suggested landing farther away from the caverns. If the terrain was anything near what they stood on now, they would need the extra time to plan and carefully consider where they placed their feet.

"What happened here?" Sadie asked.

Kaiser shrugged. "It's just a part of the world that is dangerous and unstable."

"Yeah, but," Steele said, "it hadn't always been that way. Word is, Hecate had found something powerful here. Darkest of dark magic. It pooled here and collected, and when she took the power, it sucked the life from the place and made it as it is today."

Sadie nodded. "Guess we know why the staff was hidden here now. She probably thought no one would try to get it. Or die trying."

Kaiser shook his head. "This is worse than I thought. We may need to reconsider the trip in."

"No," Sadie said firmly. "We go in as planned. We can adjust the course as we go. But we are getting that staff."

"I only meant that Steele and I could go after it." He stepped closer to her. "If anything were to happen to you..."

Sadie softly smiled at him and stood on her toes to kiss his cheek. "I appreciate the concern, but I'm going."

He shook his head and Steele muttered something about being stubborn, to which Sadie gave him a reproachful look. He laughed under his breath and she turned to Astrid who had the stone in her hand. It had taken on a turquoise blue glow.

"Does that mean we are close?" she asked.

Astrid nodded. "Yes. We are on the right track."

"All right, watch your footing. We'll follow you."

Astrid nodded once and then headed toward the direction of the staff.

They walked a short distance before having to find cover from another tremor. Once it ended, they came to a cliff with a narrow stone bridge that closed the gap between them and the caverns on the other side. Ice covered everything Sadie could see. Her breath came out in small clouds.

"Almost there," Astrid said. "It looks like those caves up ahead are where we need to go." She twisted in place, and the stone's light either dimmed as she twisted away from the caves or brightened as she got closer. She pocketed the stone and said, "Now what?"

"I don't trust the bridge," Kaiser said.

"Going through a portal isn't much safer, brother," Steele said. "This could be fun."

Kaiser leveled his gaze on his brother and shook his head. Steele shrugged.

"You both have wings. You can fly over there. If anything, Steele, you have Astrid's back, and Kaiser, you can have mine. We'll do this one step at a time. If it comes down to it, you both could fly us the rest of the way."

"One problem to that brilliant plan of yours," Steele said and pointed to the ceiling. "We get hit by one of those constantly falling rocks, we'll be knocked into oblivion."

"Then what would be your suggestion?" she asked.

Steele said, "A path that doesn't lead to almost certain death."

"Hey," Kaiser said and tapped his brother on the arm with the back of his fingers. He pointed toward the caverns. "You see what I am seeing?"

Steele narrowed his eyes on the spot. Sadie strained to see but couldn't really see much in the way of cave openings scattered along the rockface of the cliff in front of them.

"Yes," Steele said and crossed his arms over his chest. "This makes things more interesting."

"What?" Sadie asked.

Astrid muttered something under her breath and said clearer, "Wraiths."

"So… that means…" Sadie said.

"We have to get extremely creative. Wraiths are vengeful, soulless creatures bent out of shape with their circumstances." Steele shifted his weight from one leg to the other. "They will see us, hate that we're alive and they aren't, and attack us."

"Not only that," Kaiser added, "But they cause an enormity of dread and hopelessness around them, making it incredibly hard to set up defense against them."

"Great. So, how do you kill them?" Sadie asked.

Steele and Kaiser both turned to Astrid who stood with her arms crossed over her chest. She shifted her gaze between the two and unfolded her arms to hold her hands in the air. "I never agreed to being savior. Stop looking at me like that, the both of you."

"I don't understand," Sadie said. "Why are you staring at Astrid?"

Kaiser said, "She's good. And only good can kill them."

"Do you think you could take care of them?" Sadie asked Astrid.

She sighed and looked toward the direction of the creatures. "I may. How many are there?"

Steele narrowed his gaze. "Three."

Astrid nodded.

"That's it?" Sadie asked. She was shocked because in every other instance of fighting to get something they needed or hurdle in their way was large groups of demons or creatures. Not three.

"Don't underestimate them, Sadie," Kaiser said, voice thick with warning. "They are extremely powerful."

"I think I can do it with a particular spell," Astrid said. "However, it would take a large amount of concentration and I can't be disturbed, or I run the risk of over exhausting myself."

"Great," Sadie said. "We'll keep them distracted while you prepare. How much time do you think you will need?"

"With them?" She nodded her head toward the

direction of the wraiths. "Hard to say."

Sadie nodded. "Very well. Let's get this show on the road."

"I'll take the back," Astrid said. "I'll need to remain a fair distance from them until I'm ready. I'll just hang on to Kaiser or Steele's tail."

The men exchanged worried glances and Sadie giggled at the image of her holding the tail of one of the men. The two eventually shrugged, and Sadie stepped up to the stone bridge.

She took a deep breath as she set her eyes on the narrow walkway and focused on each crack in the stone and the patches of ice or moss. Letting a breath out, she took a careful step onto the bridge, pressing her toes on it to test the sturdiness. It held firm. Nodding to herself, she took another, repeating the same steps as before.

The ground rumbled around them and the bridge shook. Sadie held her arms out for balance and waited for the tremor to stop, all the while hoping nothing came crashing down from above them.

As she reached the middle of the bridge, the coldness and wet feel of the air blanketed her, and a small sensation of complete dread came over her. She swallowed hard and forced back that feeling. She wasn't going to let these creatures stand in the way of her and the staff. Not when so much of the fight with Zagan rested on having it.

By the time she made it most of the way across, the feeling had increased, and the wraiths had set their attentions on her. They were black like ink and floated through the air as though they were wisps of smoke. They blocked the end of the bridge, forcing Sadie into no other way across but to jump. As she considered the distance and the depth, all the while fighting off the urge to fall, Kaiser slipped his hands under her arms and locked his fingers on her chest. He lifted her into the air and flew her to the other side of the bridge, behind the creatures.

Sadie's legs nearly gave out from underneath her as she fought against the waves of hopelessness and dread. Once she regained her footing, she conjured her shadow sword and readied herself for the attack. She glanced behind them as Astrid continued to make her way across with Steele in front of her. Her lips were set into a grim line and a wrinkle of concentration pinched her brow. Steele also took on a look of focus. Sadie knew he was creating an illusion for the wraiths to help further distract them.

As it was, they had turned and faced Sadie, whispering dark words and begging her to kill herself.

She shuddered as the air continued to chill her skin and she struggled to maintain focus.

Kaiser stood beside her, his arms consumed in flames. Beads of sweat covered his forehead as he fought against the same sensations she did.

The wraiths attacked, slashing out with their hands that ended in sharp blades of bone. One caught Sadie on the arm, and that startled her with a rush of clarity. She needed to fight against their magic and against *them* so that Astrid could pull off the spell. The third one floated off to the side and slashed out, then turned and moved, slashing out again. Both times at nothing.

Steele's illusion worked.

Kaiser fought the other, fending him off the best he could and keeping up the distraction.

Good. Now the third.

Sadie focused on the outlines of the creature as she found it easier to ignore the effects of the creatures if she didn't look at them directly. She slashed with her sword and used her magic to shoot out a ball of fire with her hands. She thought about the purple energy she used against Hecate and summoned that from her amulet.

The creature slashed out at her again, and Sadie released the energy. It hit the wraith in the torso, sending it back a few feet.

Astrid moved into the center and she looked to the sky as a bright beam of light grew from her torso and then shot out. The wraiths screamed, causing Sadie to cover her ears. The sound was worse than nails on a chalkboard.

Once the light faded and the wraiths were gone,

Astrid was barely standing on her feet. Kaiser rushed to her side and helped her stay upright.

"Are you okay," Sadie asked?

She nodded. Sadie sighed with relief.

"Give me a few moments to rest and I'll be good as new," she said and pulled on the stone in her pocket. It glowed even brighter. "This is it. This is the place."

Sadie stared into the cavern and its deep darkness stared back. Everything she fought for was in that cavern. She lit a fire in her hand and said, "Stay here. I'll be right back."

She entered the cavern with Steele on her heels. She rolled her eyes. *Why can't they ever let her have some space?* She wanted to turn around and demand that he go back with Astrid and his brother, but she knew full and well that would never happen. Her men, especially Steele, were incredibly stubborn. She needed to save her energy for fights she could win. So, she huffed out a sigh and continued through the stone cave.

At the back wall stood a carving of a wraith holding its hands down toward the floor, boney fingers pointing toward the opening of the cave. Between it stood a pile of rocks.

"Interesting," Steele said as he stopped in front of them. "This seems like it was a stone table at some point. Perhaps someone found the staff, destroyed the table, and left those wraiths behind to keep up pretenses?"

Sadie hoped not. She held the fire and started rummaging through the stone debris until a brown stained wooden staff poked through.

"We found it!"

Sadie dug through faster and uncovered the staff from tip to tip. It was cracked and worn in spots, and the blade at the end of it seemed dull and lifeless. She frowned. Something wasn't right.

Still, she picked it up and carried it from the cavern to Astrid, who studied the weapon for several long, quiet moments while Sadie chewed on her lip and tried her best not to fidget.

Finally, she said, "This is it. But it's incredibly damaged. I can fix some of the cracks, but the problem is the blade. The poison is faint. You'll only have one shot with this. If you miss, the staff can break, and the blade will be rendered useless."

Sadie really shouldn't have been surprised. Everything she had fought for had some sort of catch or string attached. She had one shot. And that was better than none. She had better make it a good one too. At least, when everything is said and done, she'd have a unique piece of wall art to add to her war room.

"We'll have to make do with what we got," she said. "Let's go home."

Kaiser formed a portal, and they all stepped through.

CHAPTER THIRTY-SEVEN

*S*teele was used to the dark, evil ways of the demon world. Sadie wasn't. And though she was demon queen, he still felt compelled to blend an illusion around them to conceal them as they made their way back to the fortress. He didn't want another attack like they had on the way out to get the staff. And with the staff being as powerful as it was, single use or not, he didn't want to risk it falling into the wrong hands.

He felt like himself when he was around her. Never having to hide behind the face of being the demon king's son. A prince. Amazingly, somehow, she accepted him. Just as he was. Not his title. Not his amazing ability to make her melt or do naughty things to her when he was in her mind.

That made him smile as he recalled the last time. Deliciously sweet to make her go weak in the knees like that.

His illusion faltered slightly. Barely enough for anyone on the outside to see, but he caught it, and refocused himself.

He couldn't help his gaze going to her rear. Damn fine ass, if he did say so himself. Goddamn she was something else.

His curiosities got the better of him. He scratched at the back of her mind. She let him in.

Yes, Steele? Her voice, even through her mind was like music to his ears.

How are you doing? What are you thinking of?

I'm fine. She let images flash through her mind. She showed him fighting against his father when he turned up, and of using the staff against him. She then showed him being defeated, lying on the ground with the staff stuck out of his back. She showed a massive celebration to follow that would not only be for the victory, but for the new allies she hoped they would gain at the end.

Steele shook his head. Though she was calm, she was focused on taking care of his father and feeling more prepared to do so now that she had the staff.

What a surprising woman.

Human. Demon. It didn't matter to him what she

was. She was his queen, and he would do whatever he could to keep her safe.

Steele? she asked.

Yes?

He felt her flux of emotions as they flashed through her mind. She said, *Are you prepared to help me use the staff against your father?*

Without a doubt. He didn't hesitate when he responded. His father was too corrupt to change. Too far gone. Whatever was left of the father he once knew in his early childhood, that man was no longer there.

He pulled away from her mind and refocused on the illusion only. The need to protect her over-whelmed him with the images of her fighting his father. Someway, somehow, he would make sure his father died in the battle to come. Even giving his life to make sure she lived.

KAISER

hough Sadie and Astrid may have been none the wiser, he knew what Steele was up to. He saw the soft haze that slightly blurred their surroundings. He still kept his eyes on the shadows, though. He was careful of each movement to ensure no one could pose another surprise attack. Even then, he knew somewhere in the shadows, his father had a couple of scouts looking out for the very moment Sadie showed weakness.

He would be waiting a while, because there was nothing weak about her. She was strong, capable, and she knew how to hold herself in a fight to the point that even he was impressed. Especially when it came to fights with demons.

There. Just as he was about to look away, he caught a glint of armor within the shadows. He focused on the area more, straining his eyes to see there was a group of four looking out for them. Watching and waiting for the moment that their group emerged from the tress.

He smugly smiled because, little did the scouts know, they were already in the clearing, heading for the fortress gates.

Though he expected to see scouts, having actually seen them meant his father had something big planned, and he hoped the staff would be enough to defeat his father and finally let her, most of all, enjoy a little bit of peace. The only question was whether or not they would've had to fight had his brother not had the genius plan to cloak them.

Of course, they would. Zagan must have known about them getting the staff since he knew about Astrid joining them.

Despite all the wrongs he had ever done, and there was an entire book of them somewhere, she somehow made all of that better. Made him better. He wanted to be better. And she gave him the purpose that he had searched for, for so long.

CHAPTER THIRTY-EIGHT

SADIE

*S*adie rather enjoyed the peace and quiet during their walk back to the fortress. That gave her time to think. She had the bladed staff now. But the poison's strength had waned over the years of being kept hidden, and she only had one chance to hit Zagan with it.

With the time looming ever closer for her to face him, she felt more prepared. Especially with the army she had formed with her men's allies. Between them and her ifrits, she would be a match even for the king of demons. With the staff, she would take away his strength, the souls that he had consumed. She would essentially take away the power and strength he never deserved in the first place.

She let Steele know as much when he gently

scratched at the back of her mind. She supposed even he didn't want to upset the peaceful moment.

They arrived at the gates, and she motioned for them to open with her connection to the fortress. Once through, she made sure they were sealed tight and then called for Hobson. She was going to need her ifrits if they would join her. She wasn't going to force them, or ask that they sacrifice themselves for her, but fight when necessary. Even she couldn't argue that she would have a better chance at winning the war with them than without. And losing just wasn't an option.

He met them at the door of the fortress. "Majesty."

"Hobson," she said with a smile.

"How was the trip?" he asked.

She held out the staff and said, "Successful enough."

He nodded. "Very good, Your Highness."

"I need you to do a favor for me."

He bowed at the waist slightly. "Anything for you."

She smiled. "I need a call to action for the ifrits. Please have their finest and strongest leaders and fighters meet me in the throne room immediately."

Hobson nodded and left at once. Sadie sighed and headed to the weapons room. There was a belt she recalled seeing once that would be perfect to strap the staff to her back. With so much riding on the success of the staff working, she wasn't going to let it out of her sight. Once she walked through the door of the weapons room, she made a beeline for the smaller room, where the belt was. She tugged it on and slid the staff into its place. It felt right. Comfortable. Satisfied, she returned to her throne room.

As she entered, the sight of several ifrits warmed her heart. At least they weren't holding a grudge against her. At least, that was assumed as they all turned their attentions to her as she entered and bowed in respect.

She smiled and took a stand in front of her throne. She gazed at each of her magnificent people. Their fires were strong and beautiful. She still couldn't believe they were her people to rule. As they looked up at her expectantly, she cleared her throat and began her speech.

"My wonderful ifrits, I have grave news. Zagan, the king of demons, is marching toward this fortress to overthrow and imprison me, your queen."

The ifrits looked to themselves as gasps and rushed whispers collected among them.

One ifrit stepped forward, she held a fist to her chest and bowed. "What is it that you wish of us, Your Highness?"

Well, at least that was a good sign. Sadie nodded. "For those willing, I ask that you join in this fight with me. I ask that each person willing and able to fight do so when the time arises. Without you, I fear the worst. But I'm also understanding if you decide not to.

You've lost so much as it is in the recent months. I can't ask you to sacrifice yourself for me, but if you are willing, I will see to it that you are compensated well."

Another ifrit stepped forward and asked, "And if we fall?"

"Your families will be taken care of. I cannot ask you to risk your lives without ensuring that you and your families will be cared for."

They all stood at attention and simultaneously bowed. "We serve you, our queen."

Sadie smiled and nodded once. "You may return to your homes and prepare. I'll call for you when the moment is right."

She waited until the last ifrit left the room before going and checking on Damien and Mordecai.

She found them both studying a game of chess in the library. When she walked in, they both stopped what they were doing and stood with their eyes on her. Each of them hungry. They definitely missed her. She missed them too. Maybe she should let them sleep in her bed tonight?

"I trust everything went well here," she said.

Both nodded and Damien said, "Everyone remained respectful to each other and kept to themselves. None pushed their boundaries."

"Good." That reassured Sadie and made her feel better. "Miss me?"

Both of them nodded like little boys in the candy shop. She giggled.

"Good. Maybe I'll let you two sleep with me tonight as a reward?" She winked at them and turned as their mouths hung open. Giggling to herself, she stepped out of the library and headed for her room.

With the staff safely strapped to her back, she felt she earned some pampering. She needed a hot meal, a long bath, and a little rest.

CHAPTER THIRTY-NINE

ZAGAN

Zagan stood at the head of his massive army. His eyes were focused on the road in front of him. The one that would lead him to Bitterthorn's fortress and his final encounter with the queen of demons, Sadie. He smiled, dark and poisonous.

His army behind him began to chant his name, thumping their weapons against the ground and armor. The rhythm suited Zagan.

This time, he was ready.

This time, he would win.

This time, he would force Sadie to join him or watch as her men, his traitorous sons, die gruesome deaths before she joined them in their fate.

She may have had the sacred book and the ancient staff. But he had more power and strength in numbers. She was from the world above, lacking in the experience and ruthlessness required to rule in the underworld—she was no match for him.

There was no way he could lose.

He raised his sword into the air as the beat died down and feet whispered against the dirt, softly shuffling. He swept his dark gaze over his forces. Confidence and pride filled him. He had all his soldiers, witches, warlocks, and his own fair share of succubi and gorgons at his own use. Far more than that pathetic excuse for a demon queen. She was just a human, and he would put her in her place. And his sons? He would personally see to their downfall himself. He would finally be the undisputed ruler of the underworld.

Ultimate power was within his grasp. He couldn't wait to absorb every delicious ounce of that power.

He swung his sword down and the march toward the final battle of his destiny began.

CHAPTER FORTY

SADIE

*S*adie was somewhere in the middle of restful sleep and consciousness. Though she didn't really dream, visions of peace and wonderful, loving times with her princes played through her head. She had been so tired and didn't have the want or desire to even so much as move positions in the bed, much less leave the comfort of the warmth and serenity.

She knew moments like these were few and far between, and she committed herself to absorbing every single second she could.

Even the princes didn't disturb her. And she appreciated that. Which was new, since they seemed to want to claim every moment they possibly could with her.

A gentle breeze floated in from her balcony, brushing against her cheek and moving her hair soft enough that it tickled her skin. She sighed and burrowed her head deeper into her down filled pillow.

She could stay like this for a week, though, she knew that wasn't possible. The time she had to herself, just lying in bed, perfectly relaxed even for the short time she had, was more than enough.

A creeping sensation of warning and urgency overcame her. Someone crossed through her barrier. In that very moment, her eyes snapped open. The warning pulsed through her even more and she hopped out of bed. She ran to the balcony that overlooked her land and saw the shifting silhouettes that approached her fortress.

She set her jaws and clenched her fists. Zagan and his armies headed straight for her with the intention of the demon king delivering on his promise to make her submit to him.

Not today. Not ever.

She rushed to her wardrobe and selected a set of battle garb that hung on one of the mannequins. It was the easiest selection to put on in a hurry as the dress was a long strip of fabric with a hole cut out for the head, a leather bodice for a chest piece, and thick leather boots. She then strapped the staff to her back and made her way toward her door.

When she opened it, Hobson stood on the other side with his fist in the air. He lowered his hand and said, "He's here, Your Majesty."

"Keep Pyra and the hellhounds on fortress grounds. They'll be our last resort if this goes badly, or if we need to escape. Go ahead and have the others prepare and meet me at the gate."

Hobson nodded and immediately set off on the task.

Though Zagan had arrived sooner than she thought, she was ready and willing to get the fight over with. War had come to her doorstep, and she was ready to kick some demon ass.

She left her room and joined the princes and Astrid in the foyer. Hobson rushed in and said, "The armies are in formation at the gate."

She nodded and said, "Don't let a soul through that gate unless they are pledged to me."

He nodded. "Good luck."

She faced her princes and Astrid. "Ready to get this show over with?"

They all nodded, each with the same, fierce light in their eyes and a grim smile on their lips.

She nodded and opened the fortress doors.

Sadie, the four demon princes, and Astrid stepped through the door and toward the gate, passing their army as they moved. As she walked, she noted the sheer size of Zagan's army compared to hers. He had to have brought his entire force with him. There were so many backing the king, she wondered if he intended for a war or a slaughter. The size of her army was dwarfed in size, but she couldn't let that unsettle her. Regardless of the numbers either side had, she would do anything to keep her power out of Zagan's hands.

She conjured her smoke sword and held it in front of her as she reached the gate. Zagan stood a short distance in front of her gates with his legion behind him and leered at her. Sadie rolled her eyes. He must have thought the sight of his army would make her cower and submit to him.

Fat chance.

"Queen Sadie," Zagan called out. He gestured to his soldiers behind him. "Are you ready to change your mind yet?"

She stood firm with her head held high and shouted back, "Not a chance!"

He shook his head. "Such a pity. Instead of choosing me, you chose death." A group of twenty demons shifted and marched toward him, surrounding him on either side.

It was like he had the whole battle orchestrated to go a specific way and that move was the last-ditch effort to get Sadie to submit. She forced herself not to roll her eyes. She was confident, sure, but not cocky. She needed to maintain her demeanor for the sake of the army behind her—her princes' allies.

"We'll see about that." Sadie had no intention of dying.

Especially today.

Movement caught her eye from among Zagan's ranks. She turned her attention toward the source of the motion. Deseree, the succubi queen, stepped forward with her head held high. Behind her were a band of her own people, dressed in seductive pieces that left little to the imagination. Sadie wondered what Zagan had offered them to get them on his side. But, perhaps, it was just the simple fact of revenge for stealing away who Deseree thought belonged to her and the death of her best servant.

Other races and demons moved to stand between her and Zagan. Demons, warlocks, and witches.

Her own army closed ranks behind her. She held up her hand.

This was it. She had prepared for this day. Anticipated this outcome. And now she was going to fight with everything she had in her.

"Charge!" she commanded, forming a fist and lowering it toward her side. She held her sword forward, at the ready, and rushed the gate.

As planned, Hobson opened the gate to let her and her army through. As soon as they collided with Zagan's army, she peeked and saw that he had also closed the gates and raised vines with thick, sharp thorns on either side. It reminded her of rolled razor wire.

She smiled. Once everything was said and done, she should give Hobson a nice, long vacation.

Hobson caught her glance and nodded, a solemn expression on his face. Sadie nodded as well then turned to join the fight.

Demons lurked, moving toward her, taking their time. Whether or not it was because they anticipated Sadie to be slow, or because she inherited Hecate's power and they were scared, she wasn't sure. She took the opportunity of their slow advance to conjure vines from the ground, creating thick half-walls and surrounding them on either side. Though they hacked at the vines, it bought her more time to use her magic and set them all on fire. And she did so by conjuring a ball of blue flame in her hands and tossing it at them.

Their screams carried over the harsh clashing of swords and war cries. Sadie then turned to her next foe. A witch, judging by the looks of her. The woman had glowing hands of green smoke-like substance and attempted to suffocate Sadie with the smell of poisoned decay. It clung to the back of her throat, like a cork, blocking her airway and ability to breathe.

The amulet in her chest warmed and energy pulsed through her veins, increasing in intensity and heat as Sadie focused on remaining calm despite not being able to breathe. Purple electric energy shot from her fingers into the witch's chest, burning her from the inside out. The witch's body crumpled to the ground in a heaping, charred mess.

Burned flesh and blood tinged the air as she faced off with a skeleton and goblin while her army fought against Zagan's forces around her. Smoke grew in thick, billowing clouds that hovered over the ground, burning Sadie's eyes and making it difficult for her to keep an eye on where Zagan stood.

As it was, he barely moved, easily dismembering anyone that got close to him.

She swung her shadow sword at the goblin and sliced the creature in half just under its ribs. When she turned to the skeleton, she conjured her fire sword and forced as much flame and heat into it as she could, so she could handle them the same way she had when she first fought against them.

Once she had rid herself of her opponent, she searched again for Zagan. The faster she could get rid of him, the quicker the fight would be over. And she was ready to be done with him yesterday.

CHAPTER FORTY-ONE

MORDECAI

*M*ordecai watched as a demon approached him. Ugly fella with a giant scar that covered the bottom half of his face. His eyes swirled with red as he stared down Mordecai with the intent on killing him. He seemed familiar to the demon prince and wondered from where in his childhood he saw this demon. Shaking that thought away, he also noticed a couple of warlocks flanking the marred demon. He was surrounded.

He smiled to himself. *Challenge accepted.*

He morphed into his shadow and dodged the first attack from a warlock that tried to cut off a limb as the tip of the weapon barely grazed his arm. He shifted into his demon form and looked at the tiny scratch along his bicep. Little beads of blood dotted along the thin line. The first warlock then lifted a gloved hand

and shot bolts of lightning toward Mordecai. He quickly summoned a shadow shield and deflected the attack and then conjured his staff. Using it, he dispatched of the warlock by plunging the base of his weapon into his mouth and out the back of his head.

Setting his gaze on the second one, the side of Mordecai's mouth angled up and he held a hand toward the second warlock, beckoning him forward. The warlock pulled on two daggers that heated to bright lava red. He charged, and the demon prince side-stepped out of the way, using his staff to catch the warlock's feet and sent him tumbling to the ground. Reaching with his hand and his shadow magic, Mordecai used his shadow to squeeze the man's heart to a stop.

Too easy.

The demon roared.

"Oops. Did you need them?" Mordecai feigned guilt and said, "So sorry. Good help really is hard to find these days." He shook his head.

Two more piddly demons showed up to attack from either side of him. He expertly decapitated one and dismembered the next with a few expert blows and a shift in his staff.

Still too easy.

He almost laughed at how easy it was.

A sensation prickled through him. He was just being toyed with. Kept busy. He rolled his eyes, becoming bored with the charade. Two goblins, a skeleton, and a demon approached and attacked him from all angles. It sounded like the beginning of a bad joke. Well, instead of him becoming the pun, he once again, disabled each of them.

The two goblins were foot soldiers at best. Sort of the pawns of a chess game. He switched again into shadow and thickened his substance, choking them out, asphyxiating them. The skeleton was simple as it was together by pure will of its master. Knowing his father, they too were disposable, and he wouldn't put much energy into keeping them around longer than was necessary. He shifted to demon form and used his shadow staff to knock its head from its shoulders, then easily dislocated each limb, batting them in different directions across the field.

Now the demon. He had been a trainee of Mordecai's back when his father wasn't trying to murder all his sons. He had trained the kid himself. There was a hint of recognition in the boy's eye, but not enough to keep Mordecai from killing him. The old trainee attacked, using one of Mordecai's best moves, which impressed him. Sadly, he never showed the kid that he could counter his own attacks. He shifted to shadow, turned, and used the kid's horns as a brace support for his staff, snapping the kid's neck with a single jerk.

The body fell limp to the ground, and Mordecai spared a moment of pity for the kid. He had gusto, which Mordecai appreciated. But his life was wasted on a foolish demon's petty desire to corrupt and dominate absolutely. He spat on the ground and turned.

Now it was time to take care of the next group of assholes in dire need of reckoning.

CHAPTER FORTY-TWO

DAMIEN

*D*amien took out another one of his father's soldiers and paused to look around for the next unworthy foe. He breathed in deep.

Fear.

The scent coated the battle grounds with a thick permeation of putrid sweat and blood. Shouts echoed through the battle and screams reverberated through his body. There were so many bodies strewn across the ground, so many of his father's soldiers compared to Sadie's. The odds seemed to stand at ten-to-one. How did his father accumulate so many? Better yet, why bring such a large force?

He shook those questions away. After all, Zagan killed one of his owns son just to keep the throne. His moral compass didn't exactly point north. The means of the battle only suited his father for the benefit of trying to defeat Sadie.

Damien would sooner have his father's head on a pike before seeing harm done to her.

He searched for her and found her holding her own. With each foe she downed, another came in its place, but she still held firm. Perfectly poised and never wavering in her movements. He smiled. *That's my girl.*

A group of demons hailed him. He turned his attention to a group of eight demons slowly approaching with their swords pointed at him. He shook his head.

The leader of the little pack didn't seem to know what he was doing, or who he was dealing with as he and his buddies charged forward. They started hacking at him with their swords.

Too sloppy.

Damien didn't dare jump in and disarm even one of them just yet. He would likely lose a hand or an arm, or somehow be shredded to pieces. It was chaotic. This group of demons didn't know the pommel of their sword from the hole in their asses. No. He wouldn't attack just yet. He would wait until they wore themselves out and then take care of the mess.

Until then, he continued to dodge each attack, helping to wear them down. That was until they got too close and sliced him on the chest. He stepped back, stopped, and looked at the cut. He ran a finger along the trail of blood that dripped down his abdomen. His fingers came back stained red.

Furious, he looked at the demons as they halted in their reckless assault to watch him examine the cut. Taking the opportunity, he took their weapons from them, using each against its owner to quickly behead, remove a limb, or shred a torso before he received another gash.

Once he fully dispatched of the group, Damien searched for his brothers, observing them hacking through row after row of demons themselves. He found his father who drew closer to Sadie, seeming eager to face off with her. His gaze found Sadie, and she had turned to face his father. She too was eager. Damien knew that all too well. He couldn't blame her.

Before he could join her side, to help ward off demons and other soldiers of his father's, another group of demons approached him. This one more cautiously.

Now, here's a challenge I can accept. He smiled and held his sword at the ready.

CHAPTER FORTY-THREE

STEELE

few of his old succubi allies approached and Steele lifted an eyebrow.

"Oh, Steele, let us come back to you." One of them said.

Steele frowned and shook his head. He was still angry with them for leaving, for blaming Sadie for the death of one of their own, even though it was Hecate's doing. "Not gonna happen."

"But we miss you," another said from his side.

He snapped his head in her direction and noted that another approached from behind him. Sighing, he pinched the bridge of his nose. This tactic was all too familiar to him. Succubi were more than just sex fiends who gained power and life from those they lay with. They were also vicious fighters with razor sharp nails that could rival any blade he had the opportunity to work with.

"Please, Steele. Let us be with you." They all seemed to talk at the same time with different begging pleas.

Steele clenched his fists. He reached into one of their minds and saw that Deseree wanted more than just revenge against his woman, but his head on a silver platter for leaving her and siding with a murderous human pretending to be queen.

Now that will never do.

He pulled out a few daggers and readied himself for the attack. They would get close enough to rub on him, make cooing sounds, then stab him in the back, literally. They would continue to slash and hack at him until he was nothing more than a bloody mess on the ground.

At least, that's what they thought.

He took a dagger and threw it into the throat of the succubus in front of him, made a one-eighty, and stabbed the other dagger in the heart of the one approaching from behind. Next, he faced off with the ones at his sides, dodging and evading their claws while they let out ear-splitting screams.

He pulled on the sword strapped to his back and kicked one to the ground while slicing the hand of the other. More screaming filled his ears, drowning out his thoughts. He shook his head to focus and clear his mind as he sliced the head of the screamer and pointed the sword at the one still cowering on the ground.

"You were pledged to *me*," he said, voice dark and booming as he forced all the rage he felt into his words. "My bidding overrules your queen's. Harm a head on anyone under my protection, including myself, and I will see to it that your kind will only be read about in history books and talked about in fables. Do I make myself clear?"

The succubus nodded and whimpered, holding her hand up to shield an oncoming attack, as though that would truly help her.

"All succubi are banished from this land. Any found so much as a stone's throw from the barrier will be punished by death. Be gone and never return."

She nodded and scampered away.

He looked over the battle field and the utter chaos that was destroying everything in its wake. He had to do something more than just pick off the demons that strayed too close to him. Something more than just an ordinary illusion. He needed to make the tables turn in their favor.

He had an idea.

Standing off to the side, away from the fight, Steele smiled to himself. In his mind, he created an image of he and his brothers and Sadie fighting the army his father brought. He focused on all the details, which took great concentration. He didn't want anything to tip off the other side to what he was doing.

As he solidified the image in his mind, he changed a few of the soldiers to share the image of him, his brothers, and Sadie. That would give the real "them" reprieve from the constant fighting.

Satisfied with what he saw in his mind, he pushed the image out, stretching it over his father's army in the form of Sadie and his brothers charging with her army.

With the illusion set, Steele took a moment to watch as his father's soldiers turned on each other, mistaking each other for the enemy.

He laughed and shook his head. He loved his skill. It came with its fair share of entertainment. But he couldn't sit around and let his brothers and Sadie have all the fun. Jumping into the fray, he picked off the outliers, and those who tried to backstab anyone on his side. This way, he was still helping to defeat his own father's army, and he could also still maintain the illusion he had set.

DAMIEN

$\mathcal{A}$fter taking care of the next group of demons, he made his way toward Sadie. With his father closing the gap between him and her, he moved more urgently. His father would do anything, stop at nothing, to defeat his woman, and Damien would sooner kill himself than face a day without her. And it was that thought, that he couldn't stand to be too far from her, which drove him forward. He needed to be closer, so he could jump in and save her if need be.

Once he got within a satisfactory distance from her, he checked on the location of his brothers.

Steele was to his left. He smiled as a group of Zagan's soldiers turned on themselves. He stared at the group a little harder and could see through the smoke the haze of an illusion surrounding them.

Damien nodded in approval. *Very clever, brother.*

Kaiser was on the other side of Steele, fighting fire with fire. Kaiser had the fight in the bag as the warlock he fought struggled to maintain the upper-hand. The warlock lost control over his weapon and was set on fire. Not missing a beat, Kaiser stepped on to the next opponent.

Mordecai was to Sadie's right, shifting in and out of shadow form, making a couple of demons mad and dizzy before dealing the final blow to each of them.

Astrid was behind Sadie, with a couple of her coven sisters at her side, using her magic to keep Sadie safe. A demon approached from either side and Astrid flicked her wrists toward both of them, sending a bolt of lightning to each. Their bodies fell mid-step, in a heaping, smoldering mound.

Damien nodded.

This fight was what they had prepared for, and soon they would all be free of his father's tormenting ways. Sadie would be accepted as the new demon queen, growing her power and army as well.

A group of five goblins surrounded Damien. He quickly worked to rid himself of them, so he could move on to the next group. He looked up right as he saw Sadie flying through the air. His eyes shifted to his father, laughing with wind swirling around his feet.

No.

He just blew a gale of wind into Sadie and he couldn't see where she landed.

Rage filled him, boiling over, throwing him into a murderous fit. Charging, he killed anything in his path. The only thing that mattered to him in the moment was killing his father and making sure Sadie was okay.

CHAPTER FORTY-FOUR

SADIE

*T*he force of the wind that blew into her knocked her from her feet. It sent her back so far that she hit the iron spires of her fence surrounding her fortress. The air was knocked from her lungs, and her head had banged against something hard, creating dots and black clouds in her vision. The staff fell from her grip.

She fought against the endless confusion fogging her mind as she focused on her four demon princes that had rushed to stand in front of her. Their backs were turned toward her, and she wanted to tell them to stop. But she couldn't force the words out.

Struggling to get back to her feet, she fought against the weight of her body and commanded her legs to move, but it was like she had gotten cement poured over her. Every movement was sluggish and delayed, and she couldn't get her vision to clear. Somewhere, someone called her name, but the sound was too far away.

She wasn't going to go down so quickly. She couldn't let this be the end.

As her vision began to clear, she realized her men were protecting her, guarding her against the attacks of their father. Astrid's voice had become clearer and a warmth spread through her chest from her amulet. A cool sensation coated her head and she realized Astrid was murmuring words of healing.

Sadie's feeling returned to her and she stood. Zagan marched toward her men, launching fire, wind, rain, anything he could think of to get his sons out of the way. They blocked each attack and stood strong.

But she couldn't let them get hurt for her.

She picked up the staff and took a few deep breaths, rolling her shoulders to alleviate the stiffness and the ache from the fall she had just endured. She called on her amulet's magic, shooting tingling sensations through her body. She stepped around her men.

Zagan's gaze shifted to her and he slowly smiled.

Sadie splayed her fingers out in front of her and shot streams of purple lightning at him. He was knocked off his feet this time, landing with a thump and grunt.

That worked to get him off his sons and focused on her.

As he climbed to his feet, he said, "I will have you and your power, or no one can. I'm your only hope at life."

"What you offer isn't life," Sadie said, voice calm and strong. "I would rather die one thousand deaths than serve under you."

He chuckled. "So be it."

She shot more purple lightning at him, hitting his face and making him stagger back a few steps. "Look! I can wipe that cocky grin off your face."

"You insolent bitch!" He gestured with his hands. The fight around him ceased as his army turned and faced him. With a hitch of his chin, the demons charged, coming from all directions.

The four demon princes turned and charged toward the onslaught of demons, witches, warlocks, and other creatures under Zagan's control, leaving Sadie to focus on the demon king himself.

She stood at the ready, palms itching with the magic of her amulet, and the staff in one hand, ready to put Zagan back in his place. In the ground.

CHAPTER FORTY-FIVE

MORDECAI

*H*e knew Zagan's tactics better than his brothers. Having spied on a few of his war meetings, Mordecai gleaned just how corrupt and resourceful his father was. His father had managed to account for any possibility in his discussions. His generals would counter his approach with a probable outcome, and Zagan's plans became solidified from multiple well thought out scenarios. That made him even more unstoppable.

He also knew that meant Zagan would use any force he could to take Sadie down. The last thing he would do is stand by and let that happen.

A demon charged him, consumed by raging flames, though it did little to stop him from trying to attack Mordecai. He shifted into shadow, dodging the blow aimed for his head. Solidifying behind the demon, Mordecai used his staff to break the demon's back.

He turned toward another one that came to take the other's place. He took him out easily, though he felt his strength waning. He needed to get to Sadie's side and help fight his father.

He took a quick look around. The grounds in front of the fortress were littered with bodies, gore, and patches of fire and charred land. Soldiers filled every available empty space, the majority belonging to his father.

As he dispatched of a couple of more demons, not really paying much mind to who they were, he caught an open path to Sadie.

Determination refueled him, giving him more hope and strength than he felt like he had, and he rushed toward that direction. His way became blocked when a small group approached him. A witch was among them, and she chanted some arcane nonsense. He assumed it was a spell to give the demons with her the energy to defeat him then and there.

Not today.

He aimed his staff toward the group and nodded once, giving them the go ahead to charge.

He shifted his gaze behind them, toward his brothers, and saw that they were closing the gap between them and Sadie. He felt better knowing they were there, but he still needed to get to her. As the demons charged Mordecai, he saw his father release a torrential, spiraling column of fire on his brothers. They fell.

His lungs burned with the breaths he took. His eyes narrowed on the demons in front of him and shifted to his brothers who lay on the ground not moving and shifted his gaze again to his father who stalked his woman like prey.

Anger pulsed through his veins, burning through his nerves. With one step in front of him, he moved with his weapon, quickly dispatching the demons and then the witch. And the more he killed, the angrier he became. The closer his father got to Sadie, the murderous rage within him increased, and he hacked and slashed his way through groups with little to no glance or care as to who got in his way.

He only recently got his brothers back, after a long time of mistrust and distancing themselves. He just started reconnecting with them, getting to know them again, not worrying about them turning on him and stabbing him in the back. He just found Sadie and had a love he never thought he would find, and a reason not to spend the rest of his life alone.

Having had enough of dancing around the idea of having to kill his father, though he knew the time had been coming for a while now, he would end Zagan today. He would take his last breath in front of his son and die knowing who did it.

CHAPTER FORTY-SIX

SADIE

*S*adie may have been pissed before, but the fury rushing through her now was beyond anything else she had ever felt. Livid didn't seem like the right term either. She didn't have it in her to hurt over or worry about her men. That would come once she stopped Zagan once and for all.

She narrowed her eyes on the king and held the staff in front of her, the point aimed at him. She was tempted to summon Pyra and the hellhounds, to have them pile onto Zagan in a whirlwind of fire and fury as she used the staff on him. However, they needed to stay behind in case the worst happened, or they needed a speedy retreat. That was the plan.

He laughed. "My sons didn't deserve to live, much less with you. You had made them weak. Mere puppets for your entertainment. Humans should never control demons. Killing them is a mercy only a father could give them." He covered his chest with a hand. Too bad he was too corrupt to have anything resembling a heart.

The control Sadie held over herself and her powers was lost. She wasn't sure exactly what happened, but she knew she was warm, the energy flooded from her. Fire, electricity, shadow, and light all blended together and funneled out of her like a tornado.

Bodies fell around her, and she didn't care. She wanted blood. Most especially, she wanted Zagan's body parts mounted on pikes and scattered throughout her land as a warning for anyone else who thought they could push Sadie around.

She may be human. But she was still queen. Demon queen.

Zagan managed to block a few of the blows she aimed at him, but that didn't stop her from continuing the onslaught. He even managed to throw his own magic at her in the way of boulders, balls of fire, shards of ice, and wind. She blocked the majority of them, but a shard of ice cut the side of her torso and a boulder knocked into her shoulder and head.

Meanwhile, the space between them continued to close. Sadie's heart pounded with excitement and need. The need to get rid of him once and for all, and the need to avenge her princes.

Finally, he was close enough to reach with the staff,

and he looked at it with a cocky smile and laughed. "What? You gonna prick me with that old, rusted thing?"

"No," Sadie said, lowering it just a little. "I'm gonna *kill* you with it."

The blusterous laughter that rushed out of his mouth made Sadie roll her eyes. "It's going to take a lot more than—"

She conjured her vines, wrapping him tightly in rows upon rows of them. She even made sure to make the thorns extra sharp. He struggled against the vines, but they held firm. Just for added measure, she continued to add more. Once she was satisfied that he couldn't run his mouth or even move anymore, she stabbed him. Ran the staff clean through his armor and into the part of his chest that at some point must have held a heart.

Zagan growled. The ground started to shake. Fighting ceased. The vines tremored but continued to hold.

Sadie pulled out the staff, stared into the demon king's eyes, and stabbed him again. And again, and again. Repeatedly. Until she noticed that his skin started to wither, crack, and flake away until the muscle laid exposed. And even that began to pull away from his bones. Blood and ichor and sinew spilled between the vines and collected into a pool at Zagan's feet. When nothing but bone was left within the vines,

Sadie conjured her fire sword, infused it with all the heat she could muster, turning the flames white. She shoved the sword into the vines, combusting them and Zagan's skeleton into nothing but ash.

Holy hell.

She had done it. She defeated the demon king.

Her triumph pushed adrenaline through her veins. Her hands shook, and she stared at what was left of her princes' father. He had caused so much death and destruction, and she had put an end to it. An end to *him*. Elation and relief mixed with the ebbing flow of anger coursed through her body. Her throat burned from the breaths she took in.

Too many had died because of him. So much unnecessary death. She changed the course of the underworld in that moment.

Panting, she dismissed her sword and dropped the staff to the ground. Movement caught her attention and she noticed the armies had stopped fighting and stared at her with a mixture of delight, caution, fear, and relief.

Most of Zagan's army started to scatter. She figured they were now free and were running off to reclaim their lives. As long as they never returned to her land to do harm, she had no qualms with it. She then paused to take in all the faces looking at her— those who stood still, gawking at her with shock and awe.

The amulet grew warm in her chest again. She touched it as her breath slowly returned to normal. Cheers started to echo over the wind toward her.

People cheered for her instead of attacking her. She didn't know what to do. She never had the opportunity to stand before an army she just fought against and have them cheer for her.

She sighed and waved from one end of the crowd to the next. She wasn't sure if that was the thing to do, but it was all she had, and that's what she did.

Once assured that the remainder of Zagan's army wouldn't try to attack her, she turned to her princes. Damien, Steele, and Kaiser were covered with black soot, charred skin, and blistering wounds on various parts of their bodies.

She touched each one, holding her breath until she felt the air coming from their noses and felt a pulse in their necks. They were alive. She damn near collapsed on the ground with the weight of dread having been relieved. They were just knocked out. And she would need help getting each of them to their beds.

"I need help getting them to their beds. They'll need their wounds tended to. Someone, anyone?"

Astrid was the first to speak up. "I'll go ahead and set up some healing potions to speed up their recovery. I'll even help you apply the balm to their burns."

Sadie nodded and smiled.

The rest of the group seemed to snap out of their

shock and pitched in with picking up the men, one at a time, and carefully carrying them to the gates. Even soldiers that had once served Zagan stepped in to help. She smiled at each of them, giving a nod of thanks. It made her realize that many of Zagan's underlings were really victims, forced to serve him out of fear, unlike those who served her willingly. It made her even more thankful for her wonderful princes who had proved time and again their devotion.

Mordecai joined her at her side once the last injured prince was through the gate. He took her face in his hands and stared into her eyes. There was a light in them that made Sadie's heart skip a beat.

"You never cease to amaze me. I could never live a day without you."

Without letting her speak, he kissed her, deepening it, and she could feel just how worried he was over her. And she kissed him back, thankful that she had him too. And he wasn't hurt.

That kiss was the perfect end to the long battle they had just won.

CHAPTER FORTY-SEVEN

SADIE

*S*adie looked out over the land as the people that joined her worked on the cleanup from the battle. Though she wanted to be down with them, helping them and getting to know everyone, she couldn't bring herself to be too far away from Damien, Kaiser, and Steele.

Mordecai approached her side and leaned over the edge of the balcony's wall. He watched the people below as well.

"Still sleeping?" she asked, referring to his brothers.

He nodded. "Peacefully."

She sighed. "How long do you think it will be until they wake up?"

"As long as it needs to be. It should be soon, I would think." He pivoted to face her more. "What's next, Captain?"

Right. No rest for the wicked. First thing that came to mind was the previous demon queen. "Taking care of Hecate, before she becomes a bigger pain in the ass and more trouble than she's worth."

"Excellent. If you would like, I can scout for her."

"No. I need you here for right now. When it comes time, we'll all leave together."

He nodded then turned his attention to the ruined battle ground. He was silent for several moments. And the silence didn't bother Sadie. Just having him standing next to her was as much of a comfort as was his conversations. She enjoyed the quiet moments with him.

Finally, he said, "Do you ever think the blood will wash away?"

Sadie thought about it. There was so much blood that it looked like a huge black mark on her land. But if she had learned anything in her time as queen, it was that with every negative came a positive. And a huge one.

She smiled. "Yeah. I think so. Too bad it doesn't rain here."

"It does. Occasionally, when a witch conjures it or someone who can control the elements. It's just not the same as it is topside."

She nodded. "Well, maybe we could plant some trees or put in a maze or something."

He chuckled. "As if you weren't enough of a pain in

the ass to fight, you want to increase frustrations by adding a maze before your gates."

She shrugged. "Why not?"

"Fair enough," he said and grew quiet again for a moment. He sucked in a deep breath, and on the exhale, he said, "You know, you fought incredibly well. I think my father had underestimated you and your powers."

She nodded. "Me too."

"I agree," Damien said.

Sadie spun around and smiled. She ran to him, wrapping her arms around his neck and planting kisses on his cheek. She had been so relieved to see him okay. So grateful he was up and moving around.

Steele groaned as he sat up in bed. "My head hurts. What the hell did you put in me? I haven't had throbbing like this since the first time I went topside and had drank enough ale to kill off an entire human army." He rubbed his temples, resting his elbows on his knees.

Kaiser stood at the side of his bed, rubbing his aching muscles in his shoulders and stretching them before twisting at the waist. Once he was finished, he leaned against the post and crossed his arms. He looked as good as new.

Sadie was filled with warmth and love at seeing all her men together and well. She smiled at each of them. She shifted her gaze to Steele and said, "You know, they say the best cure for a hangover is a drink."

Steele chuckled and nodded. He set his gaze on her with that stunning smile of his and said, "Lead the way. We have much to celebrate."

"And plans to make," Mordecai said, winking at Sadie.

"Let's just take the time to enjoy a few drinks together. Then we can tackle the next unfortunate soul on Sadie's hit list." Damien moved toward the door.

"I'm guessing we're talking about Hecate," Kaiser said.

Sadie nodded. "It is. But I agree. We'll have some drinks first, then we plan."

A knock rapped on her door. Damien opened it to reveal Hobson.

"Forgive the intrusion, Your Majesty, but Astrid would like an audience with you."

Sadie smiled. "Absolutely. Send her in."

Astrid slowly walked in, taking in all the magnificence of Sadie's room. Her eyes grew wide and her mouth formed an "O" shape. When she reached the middle of the room, standing between Kaiser and Mordecai, she set her eyes on Sadie with a smile.

Sadie returned the gesture and asked, "What was it you wanted to discuss with me?"

The witch nodded and said, "Right. I just wanted to

let you know I had never fought beside a demon before, much less a demon queen. You aren't who I expected you to be, and that's a good thing. After spending this little bit of time with you, I've come to see you really are different from the last queen. You have a big heart, and that makes me happy. It would be an honor to count myself among your ranks."

Sadie's eyes softened, and she smiled, rushing to Astrid and giving her a huge hug. "It would be my honor to count you amongst family."

Astrid gently pulled away and said, "I'm not quite ready to pledge loyalty. But you are definitely on the right track."

"Even if it never came to that, I would still be blessed with you being here," Sadie said.

"I so want to be present for the ceremony," Steele said, bobbing his eyebrows.

"If he gets to… I'm there," Mordecai said.

Sadie gave them both a reproachful glance and shook her head as she shifted her gaze back to Astrid. "Never mind them. We'll find a way that works for both of us when, and if, it ever comes to that."

Astrid laughed. "I don't know how you manage them."

"With great difficulty," she said and added, "Who's ready for drinks?"

They all shouted excitedly and made their way down to the dining hall to celebrate.

As Sadie walked, she felt complete. Hecate would rear her ugly head soon. But that didn't mean they couldn't celebrate their latest victory before planning the next step in their game. She joined in the banter as they walked and even shared in their over-exaggerated war stories. She couldn't see her life without her men. And now, she even had a friend to share girly things with.

Despite the losses Sadie endured, which still hurt her, she resolved to focus on what she had gained: her four princes were with her every step of the way, and Astrid counted herself a friend. Those who once belonged to Zagan and decided to stay were now down below, helping to rebuild. The fortress of Bitterthorn stood strong. What more could she ask for? Everything else would soon fall into place, and that brought peace to Sadie's heart.

YOU'RE MISSING OUT...

Olivia Ash occasionally takes over the Wispvine Publishing social media channels on Facebook, Instagram, and Twitter. She also has her own Facebook page.

Olivia also likes to hang out with Lila Jean in their Facebook group specifically for readers like you to come together and share their lives and interests, especially regarding the hot guys from their reverse harem novels. Please check it out and join in whenever you get the chance! Everyone in there is amazing, and you'll fit right in.

https://www.facebook.com/groups/LilaJeanO-liviaAsh/

Sign up for email alerts of new releases AND exclusive access to bonus content, book recommendations, and more!

https://wispvine.com/newsletter/demon-queen-saga-email-signup/

Enjoying the series? Awesome! Help others discover the Nighthelm Academy by leaving a review at Amazon.

ABOUT THE AUTHOR

OLIVIA ASH

Olivia Ash spends her time dreaming up the perfect men to challenge, love, and protect her strong heroines (who actually don't need protecting at all). Her stories are meant to take you on a journey into the world of the characters and make you want to stay there.

Reviews are the best way to show Olivia that you care about her stories and want other people discover them. If you enjoyed this novel, please consider leaving a review at Amazon. Every review helps the author and she appreciates the time you take to write them.